Dear Denise,
I pray that
you enjoy my word.
I wish you love,
Peace and Joy
always. God Bless,

Mason. Isbell

A
Misrepresentation
of
Myself

Published by
MEG's Publishing
P.O Box 1555
Newark, California 94560

ISBN-13: 978-0-9823844-0-4

Library of Congress Control Number: 2009902532

Book Cover Designed by Brion Sausser
Interior Designed by The Writer's Assistant

"To give of ones self unselfishly
Is indeed
The greatest reward to yourself…"

— Mary E. Gilder

A tribute to the amazing team that helped me find my way through the pages. I thank you for bestowing me with your intellect, dedication, honesty and insight. You all challenged me to explore the depth of my soul and find my words.

My Literary Warriors

*Donna Alexander, Cynthia Betts, Rhonda Bland,
Chandra Brooks, Cheryl Curry, Arthur Cossey,
Sheryl Foreman, Gladys Castillo-Freely, Lady Decuir,
Ray Gilder, Marshana Gilder, Tama Gilder, Tiera Gilder,
Simeon Gilder, Sherlon Gilliam, Terri Glave, Tracy Harvin,
Renee Hollis, Yvonne Hollis, Christy Hollis, Gloria Ifil,
Thomas Johnson, Laura Kent, Kathy Nelson,
Airiel Quintana, Danita Russell, Richard Russell Sr.,
Adrienne Sierra, Craig Smith, Carol Staton,
Jane Sweet, Simone Utsey, Juanita Venegas*

Gratitude

As I age, I have become more aware of the manifestation of life's unpredictability. Regardless, of how our life story unfolds we must stay in the mind set of graciousness, conceptualizing and internalizing a complete state of gratitude. The reality of such a state is much easier to convey than embody, but I do believe that the challenge is to move our thinking in this direction; a foundation of having a grateful spirit.

The Gilder Family, Ray, Tiera , Marshana and Torry:
Thank you, Thank you, Thank you, Thank you, Thank you, Thank you, Thank you, Thank you, Thank you. My heart is consumed with gratitude and appreciation.

To my lovely mother Yvonne Hollis:
You have been my biggest literary cheerleader. Your belief in my ability to rise to this occasion and soar has been a blessing and I am forever grateful.

To my loving family (Oakland, Los Angeles and San Diego, Ca; Houston, Beaumont, Fresno, Pearland, Austin and Silsbee, TX; Sumter, SC; Avondale, AZ; Little Rock, AR and Grambling, LA), my beautiful God parents and dynamic friends:

You know who you are, thank you for your endless support, continuous prayers and belief in my ability to give my thoughts a stage to perform. There are no boundaries to contain the gratitude within my heart.

Tasha Radonski:
For five years you continuously purchased pencils, pens, note pads and computer paper. You also posted banners in our office stating, "There waiting Mary, you can do it. There waiting for your words." Motivating me to write this novel became your mission; a five year mission. Always know that I am forever grateful for your resilience and belief in my ability to inspire.

Mr. William Tush:
I can never thank you enough for searching the San Diego airport for my note book. Only the first eight chapters were written when it was lost and I just assumed that my words were forever lost. You heard the news and searched the San Diego airport, never giving up until you recovered it. I am forever grateful.

My Lovely Editor Joan Burke-Stanford:
You have been a blessing and I'm grateful that Chandra referred me to you. GOD is so very good and always on time.

To my Aunts, the "Queens" who held me close to their hearts. I'm grateful for your love, wisdom and protection: Gussie Williams, Thelma Calloway, Carol Staton, Rushelle Brown, Diane Conley, Debra Norris, Neil Simpson and Cathy Calahan, Lois Williams

I would like to thank my Literary Mentor Mr. Renay Jackson. Your wisdom has been a blessing.

To my Spiritual Mentors:
Sheryl Curry, Tiera Gilder, Thelmon Jackson, Jane Sweet and Juanita Venegas. Thank you for the late night prayer sessions and keeping me centered.

You looked Cancer in the eye and stated, "You will not break my spirit, still my joy or lesson the love within my heart."

MY HEROS

VONDA STANFORD
MICHAEL GREEN
MARIA ROLON
VERNESSA BAKER

Dedicated to the loving memory of my beautiful father...

Mr. Harvey Wilson Jr
November 9, 1942–October 6, 2008

"Remember that in the end
When all is said, when all is
Done, what will stand is
LOVE…"

— Mary E. Gilder

A Misrepresentation of Myself

Mary E. Gilder

 MEG's Publishing
California

Chapter 1

"Uninspired"

Intense rage pierced her heart as she read the words from a letter forwarded by a woman whom for many years she had viewed with disgust. Each word slowly ripped open the very wounds she had prayed to remain sealed forever.

> *Dear Zolla,*
>
> *It's been far too long. I must admit my shame for allowing such distance, emotionally as well as*

physically, to occur between us. I carry the blame within my heart because this rift manifested during your childhood. Zolla, there is so much to share with you; many life lessons. . .

Zolla had read enough. No justification was needed. No words could ever mend the damage caused by that woman's horrid indiscretion. As Zolla slowly opened the upper right drawer to her desk, her hands began to tremble. Still clutching the letter, she closed her eyes and allowed immediate concealment to her mother's words. She crumbled the letter, shoved it in the drawer and exhaled. She was haunted by the past and conflicted by the present. Her thoughts demanded that she reflect and accept her reality that she was bored, unhappy and simply uninspired with her life, and her marriage. Many of her closest girlfriends, especially Nia and Leena, would never guess that Zolla harbored such feelings. They assumed she was content with her life and marveled over her various accomplishments.

At thirty-five years of age, Zolla had by all accounts achieved many of her career goals. She was a graduate of Howard University, and earned a Master's Degree in business administration and a Ph.D. in psychology from the

University of Michigan. She was on the board of many local and national organizations including the Western Psychology Association and the National Association of Psychologists. She had facilitated several seminars and support groups throughout the United States and actively participated in events and programs sponsored by her college sorority. She did all of these things while running an extremely successful private practice, providing an array of therapeutic services.

Indeed, her greatest joy evolved from the fact that her life was filled with loyal friends and wonderful family members. The love and appreciation she held within her heart for them could not go unnoticed. In fact, her desk was a collage of photos and memorabilia that captured precious times shared, including weddings, baby showers, graduations, and picnics. However, one picture not displayed was that of her mother, Narvella.

Zolla grimaced at the mere thought of that woman. As she tried to get her mother out of her mind, she was startled by the ringing of her office telephone.

"Yes, Ms. Vivian?" Vivian Tiggsdale was Zolla's administrative assistant who had a way about her that was quite peculiar. Not only was she anal, but many referred to her as simply strange. Nonetheless, Zolla appreciated her un-wavering work ethic, dedication and loyalty.

"Mr. Ramsey is on line one."

"Please tell him that I'm with a client and I'll return his phone call later," Zolla lied.

Vivian was quite perplexed. "How is that possible? Your client failed to sign in and that's not okay. I can't maintain efficiency if clients fail to adhere to our office policies."

"Ms. Vivian, we can discuss this later. Just relay the mes-sage to Mr. Ramsey. Thank you."

"As you wish," Vivian said flatly. She had three other lines to answer and the UPS delivery guy was standing in front of her waiting for a signature.

Zolla simply did not feel like talking to Clayton, her husband of seven years. They had met eight years prior at a conference focusing on smart investments for small business owners and quickly fell in love. Back then Clayton was an aspiring inventor, but he persevered and became extremely successful. His earnings provided a lifestyle for Zolla that was quite comfortable. They lived in a lovely home nestled within the upscale community of Hyde Park, dined at many of Chicago's most exquisite restaurants such as Spencers, The Signature Room, Gibsons and The Blue Orchid, and jet-setted to Paris, Venice, Costa Rica, Bali, Aspen, Africa, and Brazil on exotic vacations. A small delicate tear fell from Zolla's eyes as she realized the grim reality that those past passionate experiences with Clayton were now hers to share alone.

Early within their marriage Clayton reluctantly catered to Zolla's desires and he attributed his behavior to maintaining peace and cohesiveness within their home. However, as their marriage aged, Clayton grew complacent and considered vacationing several times yearly a waste of his money, dining at fabulous locations a waste of his time and sharing intimate conversations with Zolla, an invaluable consumption of his energy. Inventing had consumed him and transformed his existence, leaving him emotionally impotent.

There was one area, though, where he was definitely not impotent. A devilish smile took over Zolla's face as she recalled the two-hour sex marathon she and her husband had shared several nights ago. She didn't want to appear unappreciative. Hell, she was no fool. Clayton Ramsey's greatest invention was his ability to provide her with multiple orgasms.

However, something was drastically missing from Zolla's life and this reality left her feeling depleted. In fact, if she had not agreed to meet Leena for happy hour at Indigo's, she would have simply went home and called it a night.

Chapter 2

"Happy Hour"

As Zolla entered Indigo's she smiled radiantly and softly chuckled as she observed several young suitors command-ing Leena's attention. Leena was a self-professed woman of the new millennium and loved life, men, and sex to the fullest, not necessarily in that order. At five feet ten inches tall, she possessed a body that would make a preacher cry out for mercy and wit as sharp as any razor.

"Hey girl!" Zolla called out.

Leena looked up and blew Zolla a seductive kiss while her entourage appeared infected with her magnetism. Zolla could not refrain from laughing aloud as she thought to herself, *This is just like Leena to be the life of a party.* There was no denying it; men were drawn to her like a magnet. Her beautiful mahogany skin, raven black hair that she wore in a short sassy cut, brown eyes, sultry curves and her spunk left most men captivated. The off the-shoulder lemon yellow mini was sizzling, showing off her long shapely legs. Her seductive walk drove most insane; men as-well-as, women. Indeed, Leena possessed that "it" factor.

Zolla loved Leena because of her honesty, tenaciousness and loyalty. Time and time again she had proven to be that special person whom Zolla could depend on. As Zolla approached the bar, Leena greeted her friend with a glowing smile and hug.

"Girlfriend, you look hella good!"

"Thanks, Leena."

Not missing a beat, Leena proceeded to give her entourage a grand introduction. "Zolla, I must introduce you to the fellas." Leena said with a devilish smile on her face. She turned toward the tall, muscular figure to her right. "This is Dr. Hamilton James Ross. M.D., *not* Ph.D."

Zolla gave a smile of satisfaction as she thought how her doctor looked nothing like the fine specimen standing before her. He could easily be mistaken for Morris Chestnut, except he had more of a Denzel Washington sex appeal. She prayed Dr. Ross's specialty wasn't OB/GYN.

"Pleased to make your acquaintance, Zolla." His enchanting voice reminded Zolla of the maestro, Barry White.

"The pleasure is all mine, Dr. Ross." Zolla was shocked by her own slightly sensual reply. This was definitely out of her reserved character. She glanced at Leena who mouthed the word 'heffa.'

"Shall I continue? This is Vyn Lee."

"Hello, beautiful."

Zolla could not think of a proper response so she smiled meekly and simply said, "Hello."

Leena then pointed to a Latino man with curly black hair and a chisled jaw line. "This is Antonio Gonzalez." Antonio thought it would be naughty to dazzle Zolla. His deep voice was dripping with seduction. "Mucho gusto Zolla. Tu eres muy bonita."

Zolla's response was short and sweet. "Muchas gracias Señor Gonzalez. Mucho gusto conoserte."

Leena's eyes widened in surprise. *What in the hell has gotten into Zolla Ramsey?* She cleared her throat and continued with the introductions.

"Sanaam Patel."

Sanaam responded in his native language and to his surprise Zolla replied back, speaking Fijan without missing a beat.

"Oh, I see the two of you have your own party going on," Leena said.

"Not at all, Leena. I simply told Zolla that I have somehow found myself in the company of two of the most beautiful women in Chicago."

Leena batted her eyes and grinned.

"And if you must know, I told Sanaam that his words are much too generous," Zolla added.

Indigos was becoming crowded and Leena felt the need to rush the introductions to a swift conclusion so she and Zolla could grab a table. "Last but not least," she quickly interjected, "this is Big D."

Zolla thought it was rather odd for a grown man to refer to himself as Big D and she even contemplated asking what the "D" referred to. However, after observing the layers of gold chains around his neck, the four gold teeth with one small diamond nestled in each tooth, and the hot pink suit; she concluded that her inquisitiveness would produce a response that might not be appropriate. She simply settled on, "Hello Mr. D," as she extended her right hand. The glare from his smile almost blinded her.

Meanwhile, Leena gave each man a sultry hug and bid each a good night as she walked toward a table for two, slowly moving her curvaceous hips to the beat booming from the DJ booth. Before being seated, Leena gave Zolla another hug. Somehow she sensed that her girl needed an embrace.

"I see you're still the life of the party."

"Just call me the international lover." Leena laughed aloud while snapping her fingers.

Zolla leaned over and whispered, "And that Dr. Ross, I could barely look him in the eyes. The brother is stunning. What is his specialty? Please don't say OB/GYN."

Leena started swirling her hips. "Yes, girl, he is and I am in need of a pap smear!" All Zolla could do was shake her head. She expected nothing less from Leena. "As I said earlier, you look good."

"Thanks," Leena noticed sadness penetrating from Zolla's eyes, "But I feel mentally depleted."

Leena looked perplexed. "Depleted?" she asked.

"Yes."

"But you look good. I see that Clayton is still on his J-O-B."

"What!"

"Zolla Ramsey, eight fuckin' orgasms every got damn night is making all of us heffas mad as hell. Please tell Clayton that this shit cannot continue."

Zolla was clearly annoyed with Leena's portrayal of Clayton as some sort of sex God. "Leena, if I have not said this once, I've said it a million times, for you to have graduated from college magna cum laude, your mouth is filthy."

Leena smiled as she moved her upper body to the beat of the music and shot back, "Honey, I'm just keeping it real. Why should you have all of the glory? Damn, Zolla, where's your compassion? Every woman deserves a good fuck."

At that precise moment a sad expression took hostage over Zolla's face. This rapid transformation did not go unnoticed by Leena.

"What's up?" she asked. "You and I are here to have a good time and you're sitting here looking as though you just lost your best friend."

"Leena, I don't understand what's going on with me. One minute I'm sad, depressed or crying. I feel stuck, like I'm out of sorts."

"Girl, you are the most together woman I know. Hell, you're my inspiration."

"Leena, how can the uninspired inspire?" Leena chuckled while shaking her head from side to side.

"I need to have my ears checked. I know the word uninspired did not come from your mouth."

"Yes, Leena. I have no passion or inspiration within my life."

"What does Clayton have to say about this?"

"What does Clayton ever say?"

Leena laughed aloud while signaling to a young waiter. "Girl, Clayton does his talking in bed!"

Annoyed to the fullest, Zolla lashed out. "Leena, I really need your support. Clayton is part of the problem. It's been four years since. . . you know. . .the baby and with each passing year he becomes more emotionally unavailable. The death of our son broke his spirit. I don't believe he has dealt with the loss. What he fails to realize is that we both suffered from the loss. I carried our child in my womb for eight months. Clayton and I read more books than I can recall about childbirth, proper health and nutrition. We even took the birthing classes and to come home with nothing broke my heart as well. I really feel that deep within his soul he blames me. He won't even discuss the possibility of trying for another child. And yes, there's sex but no true passion. When I'm in his arms I feel that he has a love for me, but I need to feel that my husband is *in* love with me and I don't."

Leena pulled a handkerchief from her purse and handed it to her dearest friend.

"There's occasional conversation, but no communication. When Clayton looks in my direction and I gaze into his beautiful eyes, I see a subtle emptiness and regret. Clayton uses his work to mask his emotions and I've simply grown tired."

"Girl, have you and Clayton considered marital counseling?" Zolla's eyes widened as Leena's suggestion was almost embarrassing. Tears sought refuge from her eyes as she observed a young couple seated at a table next to theirs, holding hands and kissing passionately.

Zolla sighed. "Leena, I feel like a hypocrite."

Leena's patience was growing thin as her attempts to gain the attention of several waiters were unsuccessful. She considered the possibility of going to the bar and making her own damn drink.

"Zolla, what in the hell are you talking about?"

"Well, I'm a successful therapist and I've cultivated a thriving practice by encouraging couples to utilize therapy as a tool to aid in the positive reconstruction of their marriages. Yet, within my own marriage, the tools are scattered and ineffective."

"Girl, it's going to be okay. I have faith in you and Clayton. Life is full of challenges. Everyone has ups and downs. Shit, I've been married twice and have had more lovers than I care to discuss, and at this current moment I'm manless but I'm happy. I love me and I adore you. So girlfriend, you are going to enjoy the rest of this evening and not focus on therapeutic tools, shit being scattered, or Clayton's ass."

Zolla felt reluctant, but she knew Leena had a point. "As usual you're right. Thanks for being here for me. You always find away to redirect my thoughts. By the way, how are Fay and Herman?"

"Herman!"

"Yes, Leena, your brother Herman."

"I know who he is. I'm just trying desperately to void that negro's existence."

"And, why is that? You and Herman have always been close."

"Girl, Nia didn't tell you?"

"Tell me what?"

"Girlfriend, last Tuesday Fay wasn't feeling well so she left work early and caught Herman in bed with some stank ass heffa."

Zolla shook her head in disbelief. She had always held Herman in such high esteem. He exemplified her image of a committed husband and father. "Leena, you have got to be kidding."

"Fay told me that when she entered the room, all she saw was ass and tits. Herman and this ho were so into it, they didn't even hear Fay step in the room or notice that she had been standing at the end of the bed for over fifteen minutes!"

"Lord, please tell me that this is a horrible nightmare; not my Herman. What is this world coming to?"

"Oh, it gets worse, honey. Herman had the audacity to tell Fay that this was all a big misunderstanding. That fucker stood in front of his wife, hard as a rock, sweating like a slave on an auction block, trying desperately to convince Fay that she didn't see what she saw."

"Leena, Herman has lost his mind. I just don't know what to say."

"Fay said she wanted to grab Herman's nuts and cram them down his damn throat. Fay's a doctor and this heffa works at the Circle K market off Warner Road, part time! Zolla, this shit is foul." Leena frowned and then began laughing uncontrollably, which Zolla thought was extremely inappropriate. She found nothing humorous about his scenario.

"Girl, there is nothing amusing about this situation."

"Well, get ready to be amused. KeKe had the nerve...."

Zolla was totally confused. "Wait just a minute. Leena, who is KeKe?"

"Herman's ho! Now stop interrupting me."

Zolla closed her eyes and massaged her temples. "Leena, I feel a migraine coming on. *Please* finish this nightmare."

"As I was saying, KeKe had the nerve to ask Herman, while lying under Fay's 1,000-count Alpaca sheets, 'Why come you's ain't tell me you's married?' Fay said she wanted to hit that bitch up side her head with a damn dictionary."

Leena was not surprised to see the elevation of rage piercing from Zolla's eyes. All who knew Zolla knew her stance as it pertained to infidelity. However, many lacked knowledge as to why her views were so extreme and un-wavering. "Leena, you already know how I feel about cheating."

Leena held her hands up as if she were giving praise at Sunday morning worship. "Yes girl. We all do."

"There is no justification for any woman to lay up with another woman's man or any man to lay with another man's wife. Certain things are off limits. It's not a sin to fall out of love; *however*, there is a proper way to handle the situation."

"Girl, I hear you. For Herman to go fuck that bitch in Fay's bed is unforgivable. He's my big brother and I know that blood is thicker than water, but Herman needs a good ass kicking!" She laughed. "Fay said by the time her lawyers are done dismantling Herman's millions, it will take a case of Viagra and a team of sex therapists to reactivate his dick."

Zolla found it difficult to refrain from laughing. "Leena, all I'm saying is that the situation should be treated with dignity and respect. I'm highly disappointed in Herman!"

Feeling the need to lighten the mood and heighten Zolla's spirit, Leena said, "Girl, let's order our drinks. You're making my ass depressed. In the past, I didn't know anything about dignity and respect. Girl, I'm having flash backs. Where's that fine ass waiter?"

Zolla laughed at her girlfriend as she reached for the menu. "Leena, thank you."

"For what?"

"For lifting my spirits and just being the dynamic friend, that you are. I love you."

Leena walked over and gave Zolla a big hug and a delicate kiss on both cheeks. "That's what friends are for and just in case you've forgotten, I'll remind you Mrs. Ramsey. I adore you. Now let's spend the next couple of hours at happy hour being happy, okay?"

Chapter 3

"Overbooked"

Zolla had to confess that happy hour with Leena was just what the doctor ordered. Physically she was still very much drained. However, emotionally, she had greatly improved. It was a new day and she was entertaining thoughts of spending the day at Magnolia's Beauty and Day Spa. Her mind, body, and soul were desperately craving the pampering offered at Magnolia's. However, after reviewing her day planner and seeing her schedule, she reluctantly removed that fantasy from her thoughts and willed herself to tackle the client sessions that booked her afternoon.

She had a couple's therapy session scheduled with Mr. and Mrs. Jackson at twelve o'clock and a session with the Williamson triplets at two.

"Those little monsters," she said while shaking her head as she recalled how their last session made her ponder the life-altering procedure known as a tubal ligation, tying her tubes. "They destroyed my entire office in a matter of five minutes."

Kevin urinated on her majestic blue Marge Carson sofa and laughed. Kervin put sand from the play therapy tray in the fish tank and Karvin threw up on her Persian rug, a gift from her Aunt Manjula, who lives in Fiji.

Providing therapy to minors was not a common practice for Zolla. However, she had made an exception for the triplets. The referring therapist was a well-respected colleague who insisted that this case required a clinician with an unwavering ethical foundation. He was most adamant about Zolla facilitating the therapeutic sessions.

On the morning of January 8, Mr. Williamson, who adopted the triplets of his deceased sister while they were infants, was shopping with the boys at a local market when the children exhibited out of control behavior. Kevin quietly surveyed the meat department while poking holes in various packages of beef and poultry. Kervin ran up and down the aisles, pushing several canned goods off the shelves, and Karvin opened several bags of chips and threw them into the air. It was reported that Mr. Williamson grabbed all three boys by their shirts and yelled, "When I get you home, I'm going to beat your butts!" As a result, an anonymous call was placed to Child Protective Services.

The case was assigned to seasoned social worker Rebecca Devant. Ms. Devant assessed that there was no protective issue and that the phrase, "I'm going to beat your butt" was a common figure of speech and had been taken out of context. The triplets presented as healthy, loving, happy, articulate and extremely bright. However, Ms. Devant also assessed that they were quite inquisitive and rambunctious.

During her home visit Kevin poured a cup of orange juice into her briefcase, Kervin pulled the cat's tail several times, and Karvin drew on Ms. Devant's Louis Vuitton purse with a fluorescent green marker. The handbag had sentimental value as Ms. Devant purchased it while celebrating her fortieth birthday in Paris, France.

As Ms. Devant took two extra-strength Tylenol, she concluded that parenting classes for Mr. Williamson would be beneficial and behavior modification therapy would assist the boys. Also, Mr. Williamson agreed to participate in an array of in-home supportive services.

Zolla smiled broadly as she reflected on how cute the triplets were and how progress, however slow, was being achieved.

Looking at her calendar, Zolla saw that she had a therapy session scheduled with Althea Jones at 4:00. Mrs. Jones had achieved all of her therapeutic goals, but she continued to insist that she suffered from depression. She had grown quite fond of Zolla and this was her way of staying connected. She showed up at her last session with lunch for both she and Zolla, pictures of all twenty of her grandchildren, and a basket of yarn to work on the sweater she was knitting for her niece, Katie. Zolla made a mental note to start the termination process immediately. She had been treating Mrs. Jones for over two years, and even at $200.00 a session, to continue unnecessary therapy would be unethical.

Suddenly Zolla remembered that she had scheduled a meeting for today with Lloyd Fairfield, the senior partner at the prestigious law firm of Fairfield, Dillard, and Molina.

Zolla and Clayton consulted with Lloyd on all their professional and legal matters. Today's meeting she planned to discuss new mandates pertaining to the revised Tarasoff laws. Zolla took in a deep breath and yielded a slow release.

"Oh, how I wish rescheduling with Lloyd was a viable option." She rolled her head from side to side with a neck exercise designed to release tension. "I'm tired and emotionally drained. I better check my messages."

Zolla's heart leaped as Fay's exasperated voice reached out to her.

> *"Good morning Zolla, this is Fayanna. You won't believe what Herman Nathanial Jenkins the third did. Girl, he has lost his damn mind. To preserve mine, I have filed for a divorce. Zolla, I am stressed out. Let's schedule lunch soon. Love ya."* Beep.

The next message was from Nia.

> *"Zolla, I wanted to join you and Leena at happy hour, but I had choir practice. I'm sure that Leena told you about Fay's situation. All we can do is*

pray for her and Herman. God has the power to bring about positive change to any situation. I'm just worried because Fay is so angry. I encouraged her to trust in God and pray. But on a brighter note, I want you to know I love you and miss spending quality time with my buddy. You continue to be in my prayers and remember that you are too blessed to be stressed." Beep.

"Hey baby, I just read the note you left by my pillow...of course I love you! You have always been my priority and the fact that you doubt that bothers me. By the way, I can't do dinner tonight to discuss this, uh, little matter. Marc and I are meeting to discuss patenting issues. We can probably meet Saturday...

Zolla wanted to scream. She was in the midst of an emotional crisis and her husband wanted to put off their discussion until Saturday. *Damn! That's three days from now, 72 hours, 4,320 minutes. This is so like Clayton. I should expect nothing less. I can't believe he had the audacity to refer to this as a little matter.* Zolla opened her purse, searching for something to relieve the headache that was brewing.

"Ok baby, see you tonight. Have a safe drive home." Beep.

"Good morning Zolla. It's Lloyd. We're scheduled to meet this evening at six o'clock to discuss your concerns pertaining to the revised Tarrasoft mandates. However, I have a family emergency. Grace's father had a heart attack last night. We're flying out to San Diego tonight. In my absence I will be represented by our newest partner, Maxwell Garrison. You'll be in superb hands. Garrison has been practicing for over twelve years and was named Attorney of the Year for 2007. Frankly, we're pretty darn lucky to be graced with such talent. He will be contacting you to schedule an appointment.

Zolla felt a sense of relief. The meeting was canceled, or at least it would be rescheduled so Zolla could finally relax for a moment. She quickly pondered the possibility of scheduling an evening massage at Magnolia's.

Oh, and tell Clayton that my Raiders are going to slaughter his Eagles.

Lloyd laughed uncontrollably before hanging up the phone.

Knowing Lloyd and Clayton, they probably had a friendly wager on the game. They were like competitive young boys when it came to football, each professing their team to be the best of the best. Zolla was saddened to hear about Grace's father; however, she was relieved that her day had been simplified. She would wait for Mr. Garrison's phone call and simply reschedule for next week.

Chapter 4

"Intoxicating"

Zolla plopped down on the chaise lounge in the corner of her office and exhaled. Her day was nearing completion and she was exhausted. Her favorite mirror was already laying on the armrest of the lounge. Without even thinking about it, she picked it up and stared at her reflection. She had a habit of pulling at her long, black ringlets and made a mental note that a much-needed haircut was in her future. *Maybe, somethin' like Leena's— short and chic.*

As Zolla continued to gaze into her beautifully gold-trimmed mirror, she recognized eyes unfamiliar, yet piercing through her soul, reminding her of the man who had given her life. She had definitely inherited the best genes of both parents. Her eyes, identical to her father's were amber in color and bearing the shape of almonds. Her smooth bronze skin, courtesy of her mother, maintained a healthy glow, and her lush lips were adorned with her trademark cranberry lipstick. Suddenly, she was startled by the buzzing of her office telephone.

"Attorney Maxwell Garrison is on line one."

"Thank you, Ms. Vivian. I've been waiting for his call." After the phone beeped, indicating Vivian had patched the call through, Zolla cleared her throat. "Hello, Mr. Garrison."

"I'm calling to establish a time for you and I to meet." Zolla was baffled. He did not even take a second to respond to her greeting. "Lloyd stated that you are in dire need of information pertaining to the Tarrasoff revision."

Zolla frowned and immediately pegged him as being rather uptight. She found herself trying to determine his ethnicity.

"I'm looking at my day planner, Mr. Garrison, and it appears that anytime after next week would be good for me." There was a noticeable pause. "Mr. Garrison?"

Maxwell's harsh tone revealed his agitation. "I'm extremely busy, Mrs. Ramsey." *And I'm not?* "Next week is out of the question. I'm scheduled to be in court."

Suddenly, Zolla remembered that her client Mr. Crawford had canceled for tomorrow evening. "What about tomorrow at four o'clock?"

Maxwell sighed. *Doesn't this woman know how busy I am? Does she have a clue or do I need to remind her that I am only meeting with her as a favor to Lloyd? You'd think she would be more accommodating. Hell, my time equates to money.* "Not a viable option!"

Zolla's thoughts were racing. "Excuse me! First of all, what do you mean 'not a viable option' and how dare you be short with me."

"Look, I need for you to be gracious and accommodate me. I am an extremely busy man."

Zolla looked at her phone incredulously. She could not believe the man on the other end had such arrogance. She took a deep breath and tried to calm down. "I'm also a very busy woman and for the record, it's important that we're both accommodated." Maxwell liked his women feisty and found Zolla's unwillingness to back down sexy. "Now Mr. Garrison, be creative and devise a plan that will work for both of us. As I stated earlier, next week I'm available as well as tomorrow after 4:00 p.m." Zolla thought to herself, *This man has gotten on my last good nerve; and why is he pausing? What is his intense silence about?*

"Well, Mrs. Ramsey, since I'm in route to your office, I will accommodate you by not charging you for my legal expertise and you will accommodate me by seeing me in twenty minutes." Click!

Zolla was furious. She stood up and began pacing in front of her desk. "He hung up on me. That asshole! I'm sure Lloyd would not approve of this arrogant bastard's behavior." Suddenly Zolla felt ashamed. She rarely used profanity, but Maxwell had somehow managed to push all of her wrong buttons and she dreaded the thought of being face to face with him. *'When I see Attorney Garrison, it won't be pretty.'*

For the next thirty minutes, Zolla sat in her office silently assessing the goals she and Mrs. Jones had established toward her long and overdue termination and how their sessions had been a success. Her thoughts were interrupted by an urgent knock on her door.

"Come in."

Vivian entered appearing flustered as she attempted to adjust her favorite pink and black polka dot hair clip.

"Yes Ms. Vivian?"

"Uh, Attorney Maxwell Garrison is here."

"Why are you whispering? Are you okay?"

"Yes, he's fine...I mean, I'm fine. Yes, I'm fine. He's just sooo..."

"So what?"

"Soooo. . . goodness. Never mind, Mrs. Ramsey."

Zolla was concerned. She had never seen Ms. Vivian so worked up. "Please tell Mr. Garrison that I will be with him shortly." Zolla noticed that while she was talking, her assistant quickly unfastened the top button of her pink blouse, revealing just a hint of cleavage. As Zolla paced her office, she contemplated how she would deal with Maxwell Garrison. *I'll let him wait. He needs to learn the fine art of patience, so he can just sit and think about his elitist behavior.*

Maxwell had been sitting in the lobby for over half an hour. *Okay Mrs. Ramsey, you want to test my patience? This will be the last time I provide legal services to you.* "Let me review these damn mandates," he grumbled.

Zolla felt that after forty minutes her point had been made and valuable lessons pertaining to professional conduct had been taught. As she entered the lobby, she could not take her eyes off of the uneasy presence before her. Suddenly, she had a strong desire to see his eyes. He wasn't facing her, so she saw him from an angle. He appeared to be reading a document. However, she could tell that he was chocolate, bald, and wearing an exquisite tailored suit; yet, for some unexplainable reason, she had to see his eyes.

Maxwell felt her presence and when he turned to greet her, he was blown away. His sense of composure was lost and he almost lost his damn mind. *Good lawd have mercy. If she isn't a vision of voluptuousness.*

For the record, Attorney Maxwell Garrison was a connoisseur of beautiful women. Zolla exemplified his pre-ference—fine, thick and luscious. *She is absolutely stunning.* Maxwell wanted to speak, but his words evaded him. He felt an incredible sensation pulsating from his groin and as it intensified, he came to the realization that the overwhelming sensation was actually coming from a place of unfamiliarity.

Zolla looked into his beautiful, dark brown eyes, smiled and said, "Hello, Mr. Garrison, I'm Zolla Ramsey." Her words were soft and smooth as silk.

Maxwell could not pull his eyes away from her. After an awkward silence, he finally found his baritone voice. "I'm Garrison, Attorney Maxwell Garrison."

When Zolla looked into his eyes, deep into his eyes, she felt every ounce of his desire. His eyes were conveying to her that he was intoxicated by her presence and liked what he saw.

When Maxwell stood, Zolla was amazed. He towered over her at six feet two inches and he weighed about 225 pounds. Maxwell was described by many as beautiful. The smoothness of his skin, dark eyes, thick black eyebrows, long heavy eyelashes, and chiseled cheekbones confirmed his African and Native American ancestry. He was simply stunning.

As Maxwell entered Zolla's office, he was quite impressed. Her decorative style appeared to be influenced by a combination of the Middle Eastern and African culture. The dynamic colors, subtle textures, and luxurious fabrics created a sense of peace, relaxation, trust, and honesty. Maxwell felt as though his most intimate secrets were safe. He knew that he was long overdue for a moment of relaxation; however, he was in Zolla's office to conduct business.

He prided himself on being highly intelligent, a furious fighter in the courtroom, ethical and determined as hell. His law degree from the United States Naval Academy, where he graduated at the top of his class, validated his self analysis. Throughout the years he had found himself in various challenging situations and had always managed to surface as the victor. However, as he stood before Mrs. Ramsey, his knees became extremely weak. He used every ounce of strength he could muster, and seated himself in front of her mahogany desk, proceeded to open his black leather briefcase, withdrew a platinum pen, plastered on his battle face and prepared for war.

As Zolla entered her office, she was overcome by a sense of nervousness. Suddenly, she felt that her favorite black pants were too baggy and her black fitted cashmere sweater was too long. *And of all days, why today did I choose to wear my hair in sassy ringlets? Pulling it back in a bun is much more sophisticated.* Zolla quickly looked around her office and felt the subtle elevation in her blood pressure because several client files, numerous psychiatric journals and various self-improvement magazines were scattered on her desk top. The sofa table and fireplace mantel were both decorated with dust. She was embarrassed by the disarray.

"Have a seat, Mr. Garrison. Please excuse the mess. You allowed no time for me to prepare for our meeting."

Maxwell was silent and appeared to be staring off into space. *No hint of emotion registered.*

Those lips and this woman's sense of style is unbelievable. I don't know what I was expecting but certainly not a woman with her beauty. Whew, I need to focus. Did she just say something? "Uh…yes, Mrs. Ramsey?"

"My office. I said please excuse my office."

"Your office is fine. Shall we begin?"

"Let's."

"Now, what exactly are your concerns as they pertain to the revisions?" Maxwell felt himself struggling to control his innate desire. He wanted to leap over the desk, take her into his arms and make love to her on the beautiful Persian rug, right there in her office. Gazing into her sultry eyes only heightened his desire.

"Well, my current knowledge is limited to the previous revision."

"I'm assuming that you have assessed the current mandates and have documented the appropriate notations."

Zolla closed her eyes as she slowly exhaled, feeling as though she had failed to meet his unspoken expectation. "Not as of yet," she practically whispered.

"And what is your delay?"

"In the past, Lloyd did not convey the need for notations."

"Well, I'm not Lloyd," Zolla was appalled. He was raising his voice to her as if she were a kid, "and your preparation is a prerequisite for a meeting with me." As soon as the words left his lips he wanted to take them back. He had lost it. All semblance of control was gone. *This woman has gotten to me. I'm losing my grip... That's it. That explains my commanding response to her. I have got to get it together.*

Pure rage shone from her eyes as she slammed her gold pen onto the desk. "Mr. Garrison, I have had enough. You, sir, are rude, cocky, a male chauvinist.....and for the record, you are quite full of yourself!"

"How dare you refer to me as chauvinistic!"

The fact that he smiled as the words escaped his lips left Zolla bewildered. "Look, must I remind you that we're not at war. My office is not a courtroom. You are simply here to help me better serve my clients by providing me with much needed information. That's it. So why must you make this a difficult process? Why!" Realizing that she was going off on Lloyd's colleague, she hopelessly peered into his eyes. "I'm tired, so very, very tired and I need for you to exercise compassion and patience and to conduct yourself in a dignified manner. I have the utmost respect for Lloyd and he holds you in high esteem. He even stated that I would be in good hands with you. Was Lloyd mistaken? Did he misjudge your character?"

Maxwell found himself fixated on each and every word coming from her luscious lips. She was right. In a matter of ten minutes he had been humbled. Lloyd had entrusted her to him and true, he was a warrior in the courtroom; however, he was not called to her office for battle. Like a warrior removing his armor, Maxwell took off his black Brioni blazer. "You are absolutely right. You were entrusted to me and my behavior has been less than, shall I say, affable."

Affable? Well, that's a start. "So where do we go from here?" she asked.

Maxwell felt compelled to mend the situation-a situation which he had orchestrated. In a professional, but respectful tone he said, "You were saying that your concerns evolved around how current mandates impact your allocation of rendered services, correct?"

Zolla smiled. "Yes."

For the next two hours Maxwell patiently explained the revised mandates. Zolla was quite impressed with his in-depth knowledge.

"You're very detailed, Mr. Garrison."

His eyes remained glued on the mandate as he half jokingly replied. "Yes, I am."

He is so full of himself, Zolla thought.

Although he had an air of arrogance, she found his smile to be inviting. It allowed her to see the more humanistic and compassionate side of him.

"Actually most of the information I've shared was taken from the actual court minutes. It's imperative that you clearly understand the psychotherapist/patient evidentiary privilege section of the revision. Communication between a patient's family members and the patient's therapist, made in the course of, or functionally related to, the diagnosis and treatment of the patient also is protected by the psychotherapist/patient privilege." Maxwell pointed to the evidence code on one of the many documents he presented to Zolla. "Mrs. Ramsey, this is highlighted and includes all relevant communications to the psychotherapist by intimate family members of the patient."

Zolla was completely overwhelmed by the legalese and the vast amount of information that had been shared. But she was somewhat confident that she at least understood the gist of the revision. "So, let me see if I have this right," she said. "Privileged information extends to all family members?"

"Intimate family members of the patient, Mrs. Ramsey."

"Okay, if information pertaining to a serious threat of grave bodily injury is entrusted to me, the therapist, by a member of my client's family, rather than the client, I'm not relieved of the obligation of acting on the information?"

Maxwell smiled as he nodded his head. "Yes, exactly. The court holds the belief that communication of serious threat of physical violence received by the therapist from a member of the patient's immediate family and is shared for the purpose of facilitating and furthering the patient's treatment is extremely vital. The fact that the family member is not technically a patient or, as you say, client, is not crucial to the statute's purpose. That's it in a nutshell."

"This is a lot to process," Zolla admitted.

"I agree. I will forward to you several court cases citing this revision. I hope that my services have been productive."

Maxwell found himself disappointed that their time together was drawing to a close. He had willfully extended his explanation of the revisions, a desperate measure to spend time, precious time, with Zolla. He didn't want to leave her office and was frantically searching for a valid excuse to extend his stay.

He's staring at me with those gorgeous eyes. Does he notice my uneasiness? I wonder what he's thinking. What should I do?

For several minutes they sat in silence, as Maxwell's intense stare conveyed to Zolla that she had touched his heart in a special way.

"Well, it's late and I don't want to keep you. As you stated earlier, your time equates to money." Maxwell's words had come full circle, leaving him with a sense of remorse. He stood staring at Zolla as he reached for his jacket; skillfully adorning his very masculine body with it. He gathered his black leather briefcase and proceeded to walk around the desk. Zolla was mesmerized. His presence was seductive.

Why is he coming towards me and reaching for my hand? Lord, please give me strength. This man is intoxicating.

While slowly leaning over toward her Maxwell brought his face to a complete stop several inches from her delicate lips. He never released her from his penetrating stare. He gently reached for her hand and she instinctively gave it. Rather than a strong handshake, Maxwell softly caressed her hand. Their eyes connected and Maxwell's raw passion was revealed.

He winked and said, "You see Mrs. Ramsey, at this very moment, something, or should I say someone, is more important than my relationship with acquiring money." And with that said, Maxwell strolled out of Zolla's office without looking back or waiting for her response. For once, Zolla was speechless. After straightening up her desk and organizing a few files, she too gathered her briefcase, her coat, and headed home to her husband.

Chapter 5

"Unresolved"

Zolla was being soothed by her favorite soundtrack as she drove onto Cedar Heights Road. She slowly approached the large iron gate, rolled down her window and proceeded to enter her security code. The gates opened, granting entrance to Zolla's haven—Cedar Heights Estates. Initially, she objected to purchasing in Hyde Park, but Clayton insisted that the upscale community best exemplified the level of professional success and sophistication he and his wife had attained. Zolla was perfectly content with maintaining occupancy at the cozy Victorian cottage they purchased just two years after they were married. Clayton, however, was determined to show the world that he was a have and not a have-not. As a result, the cottage was sold.

Zolla had to admit that the gated community of Cedar Heights was extremely tranquil. Its beautifully landscaped red brick homes perfectly nestled around a man-made lake. Various streets were lined with cherry blossom trees, lavender and jasmine. Zolla quickly slammed on her brakes as a large mother duck and her ducklings slowly swaddled across the road. Although they were sometimes an inconvenience, Zolla loved seeing the ducks. They brought about a certain peace of mind. As she neared the 5,000-square-foot Victorian she called home, she reached for the remote, pushed the button and parked her black BMW 745 Li into the four-car garage next to Clayton's Jaguar.

Walking along the stone entrance leading to the huge, oak double doors, Zolla inhaled as her senses were pleasantly overwhelmed by the fragrance of jasmine. Jasmine, lilies and orchids were her absolute favorite flowers. Clayton had instructed the landscapers to graciously adorn their property with all of his wife's favorites. As she approached the door she admired the wreath she had selected to welcome spring, even though it was still several weeks away. The wreath was comprised of white orchids, purple lilies, green foliage and was accented with purple and silver ribbon. The masterpiece hung perfectly on the large double doors. The fact that the flowers were artificial went undetected by the neighbors who continuously marveled over the wreath's beauty.

Hesitantly, she inserted the key into the door and as she entered the foyer, she was greeted by laughter. The hearty chuckles appeared to be coming from Clayton's study. Zolla was exhausted and she just wanted to lie down, but it had been several months since she had shared conversation with Marco, Clayton's best friend and business partner. As the door opened, she saw Clayton and Marco kicking back in two burgundy leather wingback chairs that were facing a lit fireplace. Their conversation ceased once she entered the room.

"Hi, baby. I didn't realize that you were home," Clayton said, after swallowing a sip of Cognac.

"I just walked in. Hello, Marco. It's been a long time." Zolla always found difficulty in luring herself away from Marco's hypnotic stare. His Northern Italian ancestry had afforded him gorgeous wavy black hair, piercing blue eyes, smooth skin with a hint of bronze and an accent that drove most women to an instant orgasm. He had it all—looks, intelligence, sophistication and wealth.

Marco grinned from cheek to cheek. It was no secret to Zolla that for several years he had a boyish crush on her. She took no offense. He was a very kind man and had always treated her with respect and admiration. She smiled at the fact that he was so predictable. He always insisted that she and Clayton vacation with him, knowing full well that Clayton would decline and like clockwork, Marco would try to persuade Zolla to accompany him by herself. Her husband was so self-absorbed, he would push Zolla to go with his partner, without suspicions of Marco's lustful intentions.

"Hello, Zolla," Marco was almost salivating. "You're looking as lovely as ever. How's work?"

"Business is good. I'm extremely blessed. But lately I've been overly exhausted."

"You and me both. I was just telling Clayton that the two of you should consider joining me at my vacation home in the Bahamas next month."

"Man, I can't get away right now."

"C'mon, you know what they say about all work and no play..."

"Man, now you sound like my wife." As if on cue, Marco quickly turned his attention to Zolla. "Zolla, why don't you join me? I can promise you complete emotional and physical rejuvenation. My staff will tend to your every need."

Mr. Unsuspicious all but handed his wife over on a silver platter. "Baby, Marc's offer sounds too good to pass up. This is just what you need."

Zolla could not believe her husband's lack of insight. She smiled politely. "Marco, thanks for the invitation but it had been my plan for Clayton and I to vacation in the Bahamas *together*. Perhaps next time, okay? I really appreciate your thoughtfulness."

A penetrating stare of disappointment crept onto Marco's face as he gazed in the direction of the fireplace. "Well, I'll be leaving on March 6. If you should change your mind, just call."

"Baby, come on in and join us," Clayton said.

"Sounds tempting but I really need to unwind. Marco, behave yourself in the Bahamas."

"I will. My wild playboy days are long behind me." He winked.

"Clay, I'll see you upstairs."

"Okay, baby."

Zolla laid in her king-size bed completely nude and was totally refreshed after the hot soothing bath she had taken. It provided much-needed relaxation to her tired body and her mind. The water was fragranced with her favorite scented oils and the array of candles she had placed around the tub added a serene ambiance.

She felt a sense of guilt as images of Maxwell danced in her head. She couldn't help replaying their verbal exchanges. She had never met any man quite like him. He was cocky, arrogant, intolerant and controlling. Yet, she also found him to be charming, eloquent, determined, confident and sexy. She pondered how one individual could be so complex.

Her thoughts were interrupted as Clayton entered the room, shedding his clothing with each step toward the bed. The inventor was definitely a pretty boy. Born and raised in New Orleans, both of his parents claimed Creole ancestry. Leena referred to him as a 'high yella Billy Dee Williams'.

Clayton stood an even six feet and weighed two hundred pounds. He kept his coal black curly hair cut short and sported a well-trimmed goatee. His heavy black eyebrows and thick eye lashes highlighted his most distinguishing feature, his brilliant green eyes. Yes, Mr. Inventor was quite fine.

He laid his muscular naked body across the bed, allowing his hand to travel under the cover and come to rest on his wife's upper thigh.

Zolla sat upright. "Clay," she said.

"Yes, baby?"

"We need to talk."

"About what, Zolla?" he asked in a deflated tone.

"I was disappointed with your response to the note I left for you this morning."

"I told you that I had a meeting with Marc. Did you expect me to cancel my meeting?"

"I expected for my husband to display a little compassion. That's what I expected. Look, I'm at a crossroads within my life and I'm feeling emotionally depleted and depressed. Do you understand what I'm saying to you?"

"I'm trying my best to understand."

"Maybe these emotions are due to the upcoming anniversary of the loss of our child. I just don't know. Clay, we've been married for eight years and I feel so disconnected from you. I feel completely alone in this house. There was a time not so long ago when we were so connected."

What the hell are you talking about? Rather than say what he was really thinking, he took the diplomatic approach. "Baby, it's like you're speaking a foreign language. The more you talk the more confused I am. My world has been consumed with trying to make you happy. Although you wanted to stay in that small cottage, I bought this dream home for you in Cedar Heights Estates. The gardens were designed to satisfy your every desire. I hired a team of support staff to meet your every need and what did you do? You fired them all because you did not want another woman cleaning your home or a chef preparing your meals—"

"But I just felt…"

"Shut up, Zolla, I'm not finished. You started this shit. Woman, I don't even like traveling but to satisfy my wife I've spent a small fortune on trips to Paris, Japan, Brazil, Africa, Spain, Canada, Costa Rica, Jamaica, Cayman Islands, the French Riviera and more cruises than I care to mention."

Zolla wanted to interrupt again but dared not because the look on Clayton's face was one she had only seen a few times since they'd been married. He was definitely frustrated, bordering pissed off.

"You have in your possession the finest of jewels. I can remember when you requested a 2–carat diamond for our fifth anniversary. However, I wanted my girl to have a 10-carat. Why you might ask? Because you're worth that and more. You wanted a 3 series Beemer but I surprised you with what you deserved; a 745Li. Yes, nothing but the best. What more can I do?" He threw up his hands. "I've given you everything and you're still not happy."

Consumed with disappointment, Zolla peered into her husband's eyes. "What about passion, Clay?"

"Passion? Woman just looking at you makes my dick hard. I can't close my eyes at night until I've had a taste of you."

"That's my point. Feasting on my body does not compare to feasting on my soul. Yes, you have been gracious with the purchase of this magnificent home, the lavish trips, the support staff, the car and the breathtaking gems. The gifts are touching and impressive to the eye, but you haven't touched my soul in ages, and what disturbs me is that you don't seem to recognize the difference."

Clayton sighed. "What more can I do? I try my damnedest to please you. You're never satisfied. There's always an issue. Shit, a lot of women would love to be in your size eights. I'm a good man and a good provider. You want for nothing. I'm not out chasing women or knocking you up-side your head. Oh! I guess that's your problem. If I were a fuckin' jerk, your ass would be happy."

"Don't you dare curse at me. We're simply having a conversation. There is no need for you to disrespect me."

"Baby, you're right, but let me get one thing straight," he said as he pointed to his chest for emphasis. "I'm a good man, a decent husband and I don't appreciate you attacking my character."

"Well, you can't deny that there has been a drastic change. Ever since our baby died there has been a change."

Clayton got up from the bed and strolled over to the sofa. He plopped down with his back to his wife, while staring into the lit fire place. It's warmth eased the pain within his heart as he softly whispered, "Must we rehash this?"

Zolla knew that discussions about their son's death were never welcomed by Clayton. He preferred to grieve in solitude. His suffering had been extensive and profound. However, he needed to understand that his wife had also suffered. How could he not notice her pain? It was she who carried Clayton Jr. in her womb for eight months. It was she who read every nutrition, parenting and birthing magazine she could get her hands on. She was the one who demanded that Clayton attend every Lamaze class and prenatal appointment. Zolla even insisted that he participate in the interviewing process of several midwives and nannies.

Zolla was so disappointed that Clayton displayed virtually no sympathy. On that fateful night it was she who awoke to find herself lying in a pool of her own blood, while she agonized in pain. The next thing she knew, she was lying in a cold hospital room several days later and being told that her son was stillborn. How could Clayton not want to discuss it? How could her suffering have gone unnoticed?

"Yes Clay, we must. The loss of our child devastated me and crushed you. You isolated yourself for months."

"To lose your first child, a son at that, is heartbreaking. How should I have responded?" Clayton looked at his wife as if he dared her to answer. "Zolla, I feel like I'm constantly being analyzed by you. I'm not one of your clients. I'm human and I have feelings and emotions. It's perfectly okay for me to grieve."

I understand that. Yes, grieving is perfectly normal but you have changed towards me. We were once so very close.

If I was hurting, you felt my pain. We had this amazing connection and now we're like strangers."

Clayton sat up and leaned his body forward. His arms rested on his thighs; and his eyes were fixated on the white carpet.

"Strangers! What do you mean strangers?"

"Two years ago if I would have left a note by your pillow stating that we needed to talk, you would have made it happen. Not three days after the fact, but immediately. And why can't you face me? We're having a serious conversation. I don't appreciate talking to your back."

Clayton lay back on the sofa with his eyes facing the ceiling. "Now you want to control how I choose to respond to you? Well, you can forget that! And for the record, I'm perfectly engaged in this conversation."

"It's not about me trying to control you, Clay. It's about our inability as a couple to communicate effectively."

"Look, I told you that Marc and I agreed to meet tonight to discuss patenting issues."

"That's my point. Where do you draw the line? How do I, your wife, fit into your scheme of priorities?"

"Baby, listen. What I do, my inventions, are our livelihood. The success of my inventions allows me to provide for you in a fashion that I deem appropriate. Honey, you know when I was growing up things were tight. My mother always sacrificed so that her four sons would have. My dad worked three jobs and still we struggled. I vowed that my life would be different and I've kept that promise."

"Clay, answer my question."

"I just did."

"No, you did not. How do I fit into your priorities?"

"You're my number-one priority."

Ignoring his comment, Zolla continued. "There was a time when we would attend church every Sunday. You know that Reverend Griffin is your mentor and favorite pastor. You found such joy in attending church and one day, for no apparent reason, you stopped going."

"Here we go again with the church thing. I told you that that church is full of hypocrites. I had more numbers thrown at me in church than all of my college years combined."

Zolla knew he was exaggerating. "Anyway, we used to pray together and now you won't even take time out to pray with your wife."

"God knows my heart. I don't have to prove anything to you."

"Well, just so you know, you have always been my priority. That's why for years I've desperately tried to encourage you to seek therapy. Marriage requires hard work and daily fine-tuning. Our souls need to be oiled and lubricated."

"Therapy? That's your answer for everything. I'm married to a therapist. Why would I pay for another therapist to tell me the shit I hear from you everyday for free?"

Zolla sighed. "You're missing my point. Like I was saying, when you walk into a room I can sense if you're having a difficult day. I can feel if your heart's heavy. Not only do I feel your discontent, it concerns and motivates me to lend you my support. If you would have left a note by my pillow saying that we needed to talk because you were at an emotional crossroads, I would not have gone to sleep until I connected with you. You have always been my priority. You see, God placed a patent on my marriage and when we said 'I do' the patent was sealed. When my man is emotionally discontent, nothing is more important. You invalidated my feelings and put off our conversation for three days. Your dick does not compensate for your lack of compassion. And as for this stuff..."

"What stuff, Zolla?"

"This house, the BMW, the jewels, the trips and the money. Didn't Hurricane Katrina teach you anything? Sweetheart, couples just like us in a matter of minutes lost everything; I mean everything. But, what was preserved was the love within their hearts. Remember when we went to visit Ross in the hospital before he passed away? He talked about having regrets. Prior to his health crisis making money, chasing women, and keeping up with the Joneses was his priority. But there on his death bed his only concerns were spending precious time with his children, apologizing to all of his babies' mamas and being at peace with his siblings. The relationships, in the end it's about the relationships and how we cultivate them. I try everything within my power to preserve ours. I don't want any regrets, do you?"

Silence.

Zolla leaned over and was disappointed to find Clayton fast asleep. She lashed out in anger. "Clayton!"

Startled by the sternness of his wife's voice, Clayton quickly said, "Yes, Zolla I hear you. Yes, relationships are important and ours is important to me. What more can I do?" He shrugged his shoulders. "Look woman, I'm going to bed. I have to fly out to Philadelphia tomorrow."

Their conversation was interrupted by the ringing of the telephone. They simultaneously glanced at the clock, which read 12:57 a.m. and tried to control the panic that consumes the body when the phone rings at that hour.

Clayton quickly grabbed the phone. "Hello? Oh, hi Nia. Yes, she's awake, just one minute. Baby, it's for you."

Zolla knew that Clayton only answered the phone as a means of bringing their talk to a swift end.

"Hi, Nia, is everything okay?"

"Yes girl. I apologize for calling at such a late hour. I have this strong need to meet with you. Can we meet on Saturday? I'm treating you to a day of pampering at Magnolia's."

"Sounds like a winner."

"Z, is everything okay? You sound upset. Do I need to say a special prayer for you?"

"We'll talk on Saturday."

"Okay. How about eleven o'clock?"

"See you then."

"Ok, bye."

Clayton stood up from the sofa and headed toward the bed. He turned back the duvet comforter. He then leaned over and gave his wife a kiss on her cheek.

"Clayton, this conversation is not over. Nothing was accomplished. Our issues are still unresolved."

With his eyes closed, Clayton turned his body away from his wife's. "As far as I'm concerned, it is. Woman, you know I love you. Good night!"

Chapter 6

"Ain't Nothin' but the Devil"

Meeting with Nia at Magnolia's Day Spa was a splendid idea. Zolla had been craving a day of indulgence and her friend's timing couldn't have been better. The discussion with Clayton did not go well, but she was determined to put it out of her mind, relax and enjoy the day with her girl.

At twenty-eight, Nia was one of Zolla's youngest girl-friends. They had met just three years prior at a book signing for a local author. They immediately struck up a conversation and established an instant connection.

During that initial conversation, Zolla learned that Nia was gainfully employed at Chicago's historical National Institute for Cancer Research, where she was a senior microbiologist. At a very young age Nia's mother had succumbed to breast cancer and as a result, Nia was committed to finding a cure within her lifetime. Besides Nia's work with breast cancer, Zolla also was impressed by the fact that while in her early twenties, Nia had voluntarily devoted two years of her life to working for the Peace Corps. She traveled to various countries serving the disadvantaged, and she always recited one of her mottos: "To unselfishly give of yourself is one of life's greatest rewards to yourself."

Nia was very spiritual and she wasn't afraid to share with anyone who would listen how the Lord had blessed her life. Now, she wasn't a religious fanatic, but, after just one conversation with her, one could feel her profound love and devotion for the Lord.

Nia definitely possessed a sense of purity and innocence. Nia exuded inner and outer beauty. She stood five foot eight, and her honey-colored skin was flawless. She normally kept her rich auburn hair at shoulder length. However, for the past two years she had allowed it to grow four inches past her shoulders. When it came to her hair, Nia was low maintenance. One rarely saw her hair free flowing because she usually pinned it up in a bun or ponytail. Nia had lovely light brown eyes and her cheeks were decorated with the cutest freckles. She was simply adorable. Men were continuously vying for her time, but Nia felt little obligation to meet their demands. She always said, "I'm saving myself for the man God has chosen for me. The Lord has already selected my mate and is preparing him mentally, physically and spiritually. And when he comes for me, I also want to be ready physically, emotionally and spiritually. Can I get an amen?"

Magnolia's was viewed as the crème de la crème of Chicago's spas. Zolla and Nia were lucky that there were two cancellations, so without previously made appointments they were able to get the works. Zolla indulged in her favorites— the aromatherapy body polish, as well as Magnolia's less stress foot massage. Nia also treated herself to a Swedish massage and an avocado facial.

Prancing around like royalty in Magnolia's signature powder pink robes, both friends paid a visit to the spa's tea room and seated themselves at a cozy table for two that was perfectly positioned in front of a spectacular nine-foot

Scandinavian fountain. The spa's tranquility left them in amazement as they both sipped on their favorite teas.

"Nia, thank you for suggesting this spa day. Girl, you read my mind. Just Wednesday I was sitting at my desk feeling overwhelmed and I fantasized about spending a day of much-needed relaxation right here at Magnolia's."

"Praise God. I just knew within my heart that this day of pampering was something that you needed."

Zolla nodded in agreement "It's so good to see you and you look so beautiful."

"You think so?" Nia asked as she smiled and gently rubbed her cheek. "Girl, it's Magnolia's avocado facial cream."

Zolla smacked her lips and rolled her eyes. "Please, you're giving those avocados way too much credit."

"Well, Mrs. Ramsey, if you must know, I just purchased a membership at the YMCA off Grand Avenue."

"Oh really? I'm impressed."

Nia leaned over as if she were sharing a dark secret. "I'm taking belly dancing on Saturday mornings and Yoga classes on Monday nights and Thursday afternoons. So now I can balance my spiritual and emotional self, as well as look bootylicious on the outside." Nia was laughing uncontrollably while Zolla appeared shocked.

"Nia Denise Jacobs!"

"Yes, dear?"

"What is in your tea?"

Nia smirked. "The content of my tea is between Mrs. Magnolia and I."

"Well, I'm going to have a talk with Mrs. Magnolia. It appears that she is corrupting my friend."

Both friends shared a laugh as they sipped on their tea and snacked on an assortment of tropical fruit.

"Girl, you know your call startled me. When the phone rings at that time of night, it's usually about the passing of a relative or a close friend," Zolla said as she grabbed a strawberry from a silver platter. "I was scared for Clayton to pick up the phone."

Nia felt a sense of uneasiness as she cautiously transitioned into her conversation. "I know, I know. Well, it's just that...well, remember when I invited you to go with me to Bible study on Wednesday night?"

Zolla lowered her eyes, immediately feeling a sense of guilt. "Girl, please don't remind me because I really needed to be there."

"Well, let me just tell you that Pastor Aggie preached his behind off. Girl, I felt the Holy Spirit's presence. Just reminiscing about last Wednesday brings tears to my eyes." She fanned her face with both hands as she fought back tears. "When Pastor Aggie asked if there was anyone in the congregation that needed a special prayer, God filled my heart with an intense desire. This desire gave me the courage to run up to that altar. I sprinted up there like I was going to claim lottery winnings."

"Nia, I don't mean to interrupt, but I'm concerned. I didn't realize that you were dealing with such intense issues."

Nia almost choked on her tea. "Oh no! No, no, no. . .that's where you're mistaken."

Zolla was totally confused. "Excuse me?"

"You see, God brought me to the altar to pray for you." Nia pointed at her friend for emphasis.

Zolla practically spit out her Chamomile tea. "What do you mean God brought you to the altar to pray for me?"

"That's just it. Sometimes the Lord acts in the most mysterious ways, in ways that not even the human mind can comprehend. The fact that He filled my spirit with prayer for you, led me to believe that God is desperately trying to get your attention."

"But why is God going through such lengths to get my attention when there are more pressing issues for him to contend with?"

Nia tenderly placed her hand on Zolla's. "Don't you realize that you are His precious daughter and He loves you more than you could ever perceive? You may think that Clayton's love for you is unconditional, but multiply Clayton's love by infinity and that doesn't even begin to measure up to the love our father holds for His children. Zolla, when you get home, open your Bible and read Psalms ninety-one."

Zolla knew that Nia loved the Lord and when she got started talking about God, there was no stopping her. Her friend was reciting scripture after scripture, when Zolla suddenly dropped her head and covered her face with her hands. She could no longer contain her emotions.

"Zolla, are you crying? I was not trying to overwhelm you. I just know that God is using me as a tool to remind you that His peace, love and grace are greater than all obstacles you may encounter. That's why He put it in my heart to meet with you today."

"I didn't mean to break down. I'm just going through some issues with my marriage and the fact that they remain unresolved has left me feeling a little frustrated."

"Frustrated? Girl, what is going on?"

"Well, I feel like Clayton and I are at a crossroads. Ever since the death of our baby, he has changed, drastically."

"Really? How so?"

"Well," Zolla paused, not completely sure if she wanted to share her marital woes. "Do you recall how Clayton and I would travel and enjoy spending quality time together?"

"Girl, do I ever."

"Do you also recall me telling you that what attracted me to Clayton was his attentiveness and his compassion?"

Nia laughed aloud while replenishing her plate with papaya, mangos, casaba and honey dew melons. She looked over her shoulder to make sure no one else was listening. "Of course, and I also remember you telling me how good he was in bed. Mr. Ramsey really put it on you. Although, I'm not Catholic, your description of his talents had me so hot and freaky, and you know I'm a virgin. Girl, I had to run over to St. Mary's and beg the priest for forgiveness." Both women giggled like schoolgirls.

"Well, the sex is still good, but that appears to be our only connection these days. I've been so depressed lately because I feel as though I'm losing my true self within my marriage."

"What do you mean by your true self?"

"It's the part of me that I'm unwilling to compromise. It's my soul. . . my essence."

Nia slowly shook her head from side to side. "Girl, you are deep."

"Prior to marrying Clayton, I composed a list outlining the qualities most important in a mate and it was imperative that my future spouse possess those attributes. I created the list while on a spiritual retreat in Aruba."

"This should be interesting." Nia put her hands on her hips. "God fearing better have been your most important quality. If a man doesn't walk with God, he can't walk with me."

"Look Nia, this is my list. Make your own."

"I already explained to you that God is preparing my future mate for me. God has my back."

"Anyway, just keep in mind that when I composed this list I was in my mid-twenties." Zolla found herself in deep thought about the order of the qualities and how at twenty-five years of age she felt her life experiences, however limited, had earned her an honorary Ph.D. and she deemed herself a philosopher of life. "You're right, though. God fearing was at the top of my list as well as, an appreciation for family. A man has to feel that family comes first. Also, it was important that he possess a good sense of self because so many men are disconnected from their emotions."

"You are so right," Nia replied as she nodded in agreement.

"It was also my desire that he be a good provider and it was imperative that he held a sense of pride in the fact that he was handling his business. Confidence, yes indeed. There's nothing like a man who can walk into a room and heads turn because all in attendance know that he knows he's got it going on."

"Oooooh girl, you know that's right!" Nia giggled.

"Excellent communication skills were vital and continue to be. To see the English language mutilated beyond recognition breaks my heart."

"Z, I know that you love to play with language but your choice of words is quite gross. Mutilated? Yuck!" Nia frowned.

Zolla smiled as she reached for her cup of tea. "Nia, as a young child I had this yearning to some day travel the world and explore the magnitude of God's creativity. Without doubt, the man of my dreams had to share my desire for travel. Equally high on my list were compassionate spirit and a loving heart. I wanted my future husband to possess the ability to display compassion and to also have the desire to love deeply. Not just the love for his wife, but also a love and appreciation for life."

"Girl, that's some list." Nia looked toward the heavens as she firmly spoke. "Now God, I've been patient and obedient and you know that I'm appreciative. All I'm asking is that the list you have composed for me is similar to Zolla's."

Zolla laughed with Nia, but quickly returned to being serious. "When Clayton and I met he exuded those qualities. We were very much compatible, but things have changed quite a bit."

"Girl, you and Clayton need Jesus. Both of you need to be in church early each and every Sunday morning." Zolla looked Nia in the eyes and threw her hands into the air. "He won't go and refuses to pray with me. Had the nerve to tell me that I'm trying to control him. He's just being selfish. Whenever I approach him with a concern, he won't even allow himself to explore what I'm dealing with." Zolla desperately tried to hold back her tears. Sobbing would only tarnish all that had been gained at Magnolia's. "Clayton is so, so...disconnected from me and when I try to explain what my needs are, he emotionally shuts down and accuses me of not appreciating him. Oh, and just last night I was reminded by Mr. Ramsey of how a lot of women would 'love to be in my size eights.'"

"No he didn't. You must be kidding."

"He most certainly did."

"But don't you wear a nine and a half?"

"Exactly! Do you see what I'm saying?" They both shook their heads in disbelief. Nia could not help noticing the look of desperation settled in Zolla's eyes. " I can't continue to exist within the confines of a 5,000 square foot home each and every day and pretend that problems between Clayton and I don't exist. I refuse to stay married to a man that I can't share my pain with, especially when it's his behavior that's contributing to my pain."

"I think you and Clayton need to pray. Please don't give Satan the glory. Don't allow him to win this battle. Trust in God and ask that he continue to give Clayton insight, as well as yourself."

"Girl, I have prayed and prayed. As a matter of fact, I'm in continuous prayer. I have reached out to Clayton and I have begged him to join me at church like he used to, but he has made a firm decision to exclude himself from any form of worship. But he has deemed the worship of material things appropriate. Do you know the other night I held his hands as I was praying for the two of us and he snatched his hands away from me and turned his back toward me?" Nia's eyes widened in surprise. "I love Clayton and I'm resilient, however, for the past two years he's been emotionally avoidant and I can't continue to compromise my spirit. I find myself spending countless hours doing the impossible."

"And what is that?"

"Reconstructing Clayton's value system."

"Well what about passion?" Nia asked. "Is there still passion between the two of you?" Zolla paused as she tried to determine the relevance of Nia's question. "You look surprised that I asked. Are you?"

Truth be told, she was more embarrassed than surprised, embarrassed by the response she wasn't prepared to give. "Well, not really."

"I only asked because you and Clayton radiate passion. I have yet to meet a woman as passionate as you. Z, you're passionate about everything."

"Well, these days the only time I feel passion from Clayton is when he's making love to me and that reality makes me feel cheap. And when I made an attempt to explain this to him, he dismissed my words. So my dear friend, this is where Clayton and I stand. He has denounced church, refuses any form of marriage counseling, is adamant about not seeking guidance from his mentor, Brother Howard, or Pastor Aggie. Nia, you and I both know that Clayton respects Brother Howard's wisdom and adores Pastor Aggie." Zolla collapsed back into her chair as she slowly turned her attention to the calm waters flowing from the huge fountain. She sighed. "Nia, what am I to do?"

"Instead of giving you my opinion, I'm going to provide you with the direct line to my therapist," Nia said as she smiled proudly.

Zolla's jaw dropped in surprise. "Nia, I didn't know you were in therapy."

"Yep, three hundred and sixty-five days a year, seven days a week and twenty-four hours a day until the day I die. When I say my therapist, I'm referring to our Father and unlike you, He accepts all insurance plans."

Zolla chuckled "Is that so?"

"Yes indeed," Nia boasted. "I know that God has a plan for you. I'm certain that everything taking place right now is aligned with that plan. The fact that you are His daughter lets me know that he is going to take care of you and never lead you astray. My only advice for you is to be still and trust in who He is."

"Uh, that's what I've been doing."

Nia cautiously returned her tea cup to its saucer. She leaned back into her chair as she tenderly looked directly into the almond-shaped eyes facing her. "Zolla Naria Ramsey, not only do you need to be still, you need to quiet yourself so that you can hear God's direction. Be submissive to His voice."

"I understand what you're saying, but at this point I just feel so discouraged. I can't even say for certain that the continuance of my marriage is important to me. You know, I'm just tired. As a matter of fact, the strangest thing happened to me on Wednesday that has left me with the most awkward feeling. I just have to share it with someone. I can't hold it in."

Nia, bursting at the seams with curiosity, leaned over and whispered, "Well, judging from that sparkle in your eyes, it must be something juicy, so spill it!"

Zolla took a deep breath and began wringing her hands nervously. "I just don't know how to express this. I feel so uncomfortable. Okay wait, why are you giving me that get-to-the-point expression?"

"Because I want you to get to the point. Stop acting shy and reserved. Just tell me."

"Okay, here I go. Wednesday evening, Lloyd and I were scheduled to meet, but he left me a message that we needed to reschedule due to Grace's father's sudden health crisis. He said that the firm's newest partner, Maxwell Garrison, would be representing him and that I should anticipate his telephone call for the rescheduling of our meeting."

"Are you talking about Kevin-Costner-look-a-like Lloyd?"

"Nia Denise, are you still drooling over that man? Girl, Grace has no tolerance when it comes to Lloyd and his female fan club. She might appear high society but she can get ghetto."

"Zolla, please! But if I wasn't saved, sanctified and highly favored, I just might challenge Mrs. Fairfield; give her a run for her money and Lloyd's too." They both cracked up.

"Anyways, Mr. Garrison, or should I say Attorney Maxwell Garrison, phoned my office several hours later and was extremely unprofessional, a real piece of work."

"What do you mean by a piece of work?"

"Well, he was rude and cocky, insisting that I accommodate him. I tell you our conversation was equivalent to something you'd see in a movie. He definitely fit the profile of an arrogant and chauvinistic attorney. And girl, he's a brother. Can you believe that?"

"Why was that a shock?" Nia asked. " Zar, and Warner are your friends and both are highly accomplished black lawyers."

"It was his voice. His tone Just his tone alone said 'I think I'm better than you', so I just assumed that he was Caucasian. I would have never guessed that he was black. Anyway, just before ending our conversation, he had the audacity to inform me that he was in route to my office and that I should be prepared to meet with him in twenty minutes."

Nia's mouth hung wide open for at least ten seconds as she tried to digest Zolla's words. "He hung up on you? Now this is one situation where you wouldn't have to worry about me getting on you for losing your religion. You did lose your religion on him, didn't you?"

"Girl, that was my intention. I was livid. But when I walked into that lobby and my eyes settled on him, I needed every ounce of religion I could muster. I can't explain it. He had me speechless for a moment."

Nia looked confused. "So, you went from livid to admiration in a matter of seconds?"

Zolla nodded in agreement. "Exactly and I'm also at a loss for a rational explanation. To make matters worse, for some strange reason I had to see his eyes."

Mary E. Gilder

"His eyes?"

"Yes, his eyes. I had this strong desire to see his eyes and when he turned to greet me and our eyes connected, I could feel his reaction to me. Instant attraction emanated from his eyes."

Nia shrugged her shoulders? "So, what makes this situation unique? You're a beautiful woman and men are always drooling over you."

"Well, we spent over two hours in my office discussing legal mandates and during the entire time I could feel his strong desire for me. I felt his eyes betraying him; letting me know that at that very moment he had fallen weak for me and that I'd had an effect on him."

Nia folded her arms. She could smell trouble brewing. "Humph" she said.

"What do you mean by humph? Don't humph me."

"And again I ask, what makes this situation any different from the others?"

"There has only been one other time in my life when I can recall being confronted with this... these unexplainable feelings."

"And when was that?"

She was slow to respond. "When I met Clayton, Maxwell had the same effect on me. I can't deny it. I can't erase him from my thoughts."

"So you mean to tell me that you are lusting after another man? Are you aware that lust is the culprit of many sins?"

"Yes, I know, but I'm not lusting." *Here we go again, the start of another Holy War. Why did I open my mouth?*" she thought.

"Zolla, you of all people. You are a married woman and you have always made it crystal clear—"

Zolla interrupted. "Made what crystal clear?"

"How you feel about adultery. I mean you've ended friendships with close friends after they disclosed to you their involvement with unavailable men."

Zolla appeared to have had a lapse in memory. "I beg your pardon."

Nia rattled off the names like a grocery list. "Connie, Phyllis and Gabriella."

"Well, that was different."

"How? Do tell. This should be fascinating."

"Well, Connie was sleeping with her husband's boss and Phyllis was having sex with her married chiropractor every Tuesday and Thursday at 2:30 p.m. and bragged about it.

Said that her back was finally aligned. And Gabriella's situation still brothers me because she came to me and shared how she and Gustavo were contemplating divorce. I suggested marital counseling. I never told her to sleep with her therapist. Not only did they have an affair for over a year, but she had the man's baby."

"But Zolla, you had the man's license revoked."

"Yes I did. Dr. Bradford Wilson had been in private practice for over twenty years and he had a code of ethics to uphold and he crossed the line. Gustavo and Gabriella met with Dr. Wilson regularly. Poor Gustavo trusted that Dr. Wilson's interventions were in the best interests of his marriage. But for an entire year, his therapist was having an affair with his wife. Oh, you best believe I reported Bradford's unethical butt. Wait a minute, I know you don't support Gabriella's behavior?"

"Zolla, when Gabriella came to you she was practically out of her mind. She was in need of your support. She was pregnant and her family, out of shame, had disowned her. Gabriella came to you for help."

"Okay, what should have been my reaction since you have all of the answers?"

"The least you could have done was to remind her of God's love for her and you could have prayed with her, but instead you allowed your rigid values to exceed God's love and mercy. You forgot to tell Gabriella that God is a forgiving God. That's what you forgot to do. She simply came to you for advice and you turned your back on her. I never understood your reaction, especially since you're a therapist." Zolla rolled her eyes as if she was getting bored with Nia's tirade. "All I'm saying is that I find it ironic that you showed no tolerance to their situations, and it now appears that Miss Rigid and Overly Judgmental has become a victim of her own ridicule."

Zolla felt that her character was being attacked. "Goodness Nia, I'm not saying that I want to sleep with the man."

"That may not be your intention but Satan knows that at this very moment your relationship with Clayton is extremely fragile and that he's emotionally unavailable. So, what better way to destroy your marriage than making this Maxwell Garrison available to you?"

Zolla thought to herself, "*I don't believe this. I really don't believe this. Why did I open my mouth?*"

101

"Nia, all I'm saying is that something unexplainable happened between Maxwell and I. Be assured that it wasn't lust or a sexual desire; it was something more profound."

"Okay and all I'm saying is that you better stay prayerful because a one-way ticket to hell is cheap and will last an eternity. I know game when I see it and this situation has Satan's stamp of approval written all over it. This ain't nothin' but the devil playing chess with your soul. And if you let him play too long, he just might yell checkmate." Nia stood up and walked over to her friend with arms extended. "Girl, give me a hug." As they embraced, Nia closed her eyes and whispered softly into Zolla's right ear. "Zolla, I love you so much and if you don't ever listen to another word I say, please take heed to these words: This ain't nothin' but the devil, nothin' but the devil."

Chapter 7

"Unfinished Business"

Two months had passed since Zolla's spa day with Nia, whose powerful departing words "*nothing but the devil*" continuously replayed in Zolla's mind. She had tried dismissing all conscious thoughts of Maxwell Garrison, but it was no easy task because the only coping mechanism she employed was her own will power. But once she turned to God and prayed for his continued guidance and strength, her desire to see Maxwell lessened. Unsettling, though, was the feeling deep within her soul that reminded her spirit that there was unfinished business between she and the sexy attorney.

Meanwhile, the dysfunction within her marriage continued. Clayton's emotional unavailability seemed indefinite, as he consumed himself with endless special projects. To one's watchful eye, it appeared that he had created a world where he and only he existed. He only physically returned for the consumption of food, the closing of a deal and of course, the pleasure of lovemaking. Zolla found temporary solace by keeping busy at work with frequent speaking engagements and by assisting her Nanna with the upcoming family reunion. She was looking forward to the family gathering because it had been years since she had spent time with her only sibling, her younger brother, Zion. He and his wife Teresa had four precious daughters: Shelby who was 8, Maddison, who just turned 6, Isabella, the four year old and Veronica who was 2. Spoiling her nieces rotten brought Zolla a tremendous amount of joy. She had spent the last few weeks consumed with the purchasing of dresses, shoes, jewelry and purses for the four princesses. Of course, each purchase would be wrapped with Zolla's trademark eloquence and presented to each girl during their visit.

This year, Nanna, the white haired, 80-year-old matriarch of the family had assigned Zolla the task of event coordination and Zolla was determined to present her family with an array of spectacular, fun-filled activities. As she brainstormed and added items to her checklist, she was interrupted by an urgent knock on her office door.

"Yes, Ms. Vivian?"

Vivian entered appearing frantic. There was a sense of urgency in her voice. "He. . . he's here," she stuttered.

Zolla's thoughts were racing. *My God, it can't be. This can't be happening.* She prayed that the words coming from Vivian's mouth would prove her thoughts wrong.

"Uh, who's here?" she asked.

Vivian smirked. "Attorney Garrison."

Zolla's heart skipped a beat as her level of anxiety quickly elevated. She had been avoiding his telephone calls for the past two months and she gave Vivian strict instruction to send him away if he were to show up unannounced.

"Well, did you handle the situation?"

"Of course I did. I told him the usual, that you were out of town."

"And what was his response?"

"I don't think he bought it."

"What makes you say that?"

"Well, he took a few steps towards the door, stopped for about ten seconds, turned and proceeded to take a couple steps towards me and came to a complete stop. He smiled while shaking his head from side to side as he stared directly into my eyes."

Zolla stepped away from her desk and slowly walked toward the large blue sofa and sought refuge in the comfort of its large pillows. She looked at Vivian with desperation.

"Did he go away, Ms. Vivian? Please tell me that he's gone."

"Yes, he's gone."

Zolla closed her eyes and sighed.

"Zolla, I don't mean to pry, but why all of the theatrics? Why can't you simply confront this man? Should I be concerned? Has he been inappropriate with you?"

"Absolutely not," Zolla was shocked that Vivian would even think such a thing. "It's not a simple situation. In fact, it's extremely complex. I don't feel like discussing it right now. Maybe later, okay?"

Much like a mother's intuition, Vivian felt as though something still wasn't quite right. Thoughts flooded her mind. *Zolla has had me jumping through hoops to keep this man away from her and I'm starting to get worried.*

"Is there anything else, Zolla?"

"Just a word of thanks. And Ms. Vivian, I do appreciate all that you do for me."

"Zolla, it's Vivian."

"Pardon?" Zolla squinted her eyes in confusion.

"Since the day you hired me you insisted that I refer to you as Zolla. Now, I think it's time you refer to me as Vivian."

Zolla hesitated a bit due to the fact that Ms. Vivian was twenty-five years her senior, and her Nanna McKenzie had taught her always to respect her elders.

"Uh, okay, Ms., I mean, Vivian, but this will be an adjustment for me. Oh, when my Nanna is present, out of respect for her, I must refer to you as Ms. Vivian."

"Not a problem," Vivian chuckled and then quickly displayed a serious look. "You might find this extremely difficult to believe..."

"Find what difficult to believe, Vivian?"

"That some people find me somewhat peculiar and controlling." Zolla knew she was one of those 'some people' but she wouldn't dare insult Vivian. She simply acted surprised.

"What?"

"Yeah, but Zolla, you have always made me feel valued and appreciated. Be assured of this, sweetie, I will always look out for your best interests, always."

Zolla was touched. It was rare for Vivian to display such emotion. It was rather comforting to be reassured of her protectiveness. As Vivian left her office, Zolla's thoughts were conflicted. For the life of her she could not understand why Maxwell Garrison was being so persistent. Suddenly she heard heavy footsteps coming toward her office and Vivian's elevated voice.

"You cannot go in there," Vivian demanded. "I've already explained to you that Mrs. Ramsey is out of town." The door to Zolla's office swung open and Vivian slipped in, quickly closing the door behind her. She was speaking so fast that she was nearly out of breath.

"I told him that you were not in, but he refused to listen. I tell you, that man is determined. Zolla, I did my very best to contain him but. . ."

Before Vivian could complete her sentence, the door to Zolla's office opened and Maxwell strutted right in like a peacock showing its feathers. He glared confidently at Zolla and boldly said, "Ms. Tiggsdale, is it? Didn't Mrs. Ramsey inform you that I cannot be contained? From the moment I entered your office this morning, I knew Mrs. Ramsey was here" He turned to Zolla. "The entire office is scented with your tantalizing perfume."

Zolla shook her head and matched his confident stare with one of her own. "So, Mr. Garrison, if it's true about my intoxicating fragrance..."

Her words were quickly interrupted. "Mrs. Ramsey, you misquoted me. I referred to your fragrance as tantalizing. However, I find *you* to be very much intoxicating." All Zolla could say to herself was damn. She was caught off guard, but he would never know it.

"As I was saying Mr. Garrison, if my fragrance led you to believe that I was here, why did you leave my office earlier?"

Zolla wore a smirk of satisfaction. She had put him in the hot seat.

"Well, Mrs. Ramsey, if you must know, I knew that your assistant would tell you that I came by. So I decided to go across the street for a cup of coffee and read the morning paper. That would allow for much needed time. . ."

"Time for what?"

"For you to properly prepare for me, for my return."

Zolla was speechless as Maxwell smiled, turning his attention to Vivian, who had been watching their back and forth exchange. All she needed was a diet ginger ale and her favorite popcorn with extra butter. The dialogue between Zolla and Maxwell was far more intriguing than any movie she had watched in the last year.

"Ms. Tiggsdale," he said sincerely, "I apologize if my behavior has in any way compromised you. However, I've concluded that there is unfinished business between Mrs. Ramsey and myself."

Zolla desperately tried but she had failed. She could not lure her eyes away from him. He was dressed exquisitely in a navy blue suit, white shirt, and a blue tie with red and white accents. The suit was definitely wearing him. The silver cuff links and the massive silver Rolex watch made him look like a GQ model. It wasn't as though she was unaccustomed to designer fashion, but in this case, Maxwell made the fashion look like a million bucks. And he had the audacity to be wearing her favorite Jean Paul Gaultier cologne. Vivian appeared to be in a hypnotic trance. She was practically drooling at the mouth. Zolla realized that she was staring at Maxwell like he was a one-of-a-kind work of art at a museum. She immediately sat down behind the security of her massive desk. She was making sure there was distance between she and Mr. Garrison.

"Vivian," Zolla called.

Silence.

"Vivian," she repeated. Still no reply.

Zolla enunciated every syllable in her name. "Viv-i-an."

Snapping out of it, Vivian was startled. "Yes Mrs. Ramsey? I mean Zolla."

"You can leave. I will be fine. Just take the remainder of the day off okay?"

"Thank you, Zolla. Good day, Mr. Garrison." She nodded in his direction.

"Good day, Ms. Tiggsdale," he said and winked. As Vivian left the office, Maxwell took a seat, reacquainting himself with the black leather chair positioned in front of the massive mahogany desk, successfully adding separation from him and the source of his escalating desire.

"Mrs. Ramsey, you are quite the challenge. I have spent the last eight weeks trying to contact you to no avail." Zolla felt her level of comfort lessening as she sought strength and reassurance from Nia's words.

She cleared her throat. "I've been extremely busy."

He slowly nodded his head. "I see, I see."

"Mr. Garrison, why are you here? Our business is finished."

"Quite the contrary. I don't believe it is. Mrs. Ramsey, I have left over ten messages for you this month alone and I've been to your office on four different occasions." He straightened his tie and continued in his closing argument voice. "For the record, I only reserve such attention for clients paying me over one-thousand dollars per hour. I, as of yet, have failed to ascertain as to why your assistant would allow for me to be seated facing her for over ten minutes before notifying me of your unavailability."

Zolla knew and understood Vivian's need to sneak a few minutes alone with this man. He had apparently not looked at his reflection in a mirror lately. Yes, Vivian was rather odd but she was still a woman.

"I'm no fool, Mrs. Ramsey."

Zolla needed to respond. She had to. "Mr. Garrison, I never stated..."

"Were you captivated by the seven dozen red roses I had delivered to you?" he asked with a devilish grin.

Zolla was suddenly light headed.

"Are you okay?"

No she wasn't ok. Clayton had been out of town and prior to his departure they had their usual argument. When the roses arrived yesterday, she didn't even read the attached message and just assumed they were from him.

Trying to regain her composure Zolla said, "I'm fine. I was just unaware that they were from you." Maxwell crossed his leg and brought his right hand to rest under his chin.

"Mrs. Ramsey?"

"Yes?" For some reason him referring to her as Mrs. Ramsey made her feel ancient.

"Call me Zolla, okay?"

"Done."

"And call me Maxwell." Zolla rolled her eyes, remembering how she had just shared the same conversation with Vivian. She was quickly losing patience with him.

"Listen Maxwell, what in the hell do you want? Why are you here? She spat. In her mind, there was truly nothing left to discuss with the man.

Maxwell simply gave her a half-hearted smile and continued the conversation with this woman he found to be fascinating. "Zolla, did I ever share with you that in my prime I was quite the ladies' man?"

Zolla stared at him incredulously. "No, I know nothing about your personal life nor do I see a need for you to divulge. We're not friends."

Maxwell quickly dismissed her words. "Shall I continue? After graduating from Annapolis I traveled the world. My employer at that time, the U.S. Navy, mandated that I practice law on various naval bases all over the world. Every where my travels took me, I sampled the women. I was a connoisseur of exotic women." Zolla was feeling a sense of increased repulsion, as she came to the realization that in her office sitting before her was a whore.

Your dick must be exhausted, she thought. But her conscious would not permit such bluntness, so she settled on language a little less cruel. "Well, you must be exhausted," she said sarcastically. "And what does this have to do with me? I have no desire to hear about your many sexual conquests."

"Okay, here's the thing, during my period of mass consumption, I was a married man."

"Uh, we really need to bring this conversation to closure and I'm asking that you leave my office, now!"

He had willfully sought her out so he could get this off his chest. He was determined to complete his mission and he was not about to turn and walk away from her.

"No, Zolla! Just listen. I beg you. Trust me. This is all relevant, okay?" As wary as she was, Zolla decided to go against her instincts.

"Okay, Maxwell. Just make it quick."

"When I was married, it wasn't for love, it was for lust. She was extremely attractive and very successful. Physically, as a couple, we were pleasing to the eye. Emotionally, we were unevenly yoked. I grew complacent and increasingly found myself seeking out solitude, love and validation of my manhood within the wombs of countless women."

Zolla sighed. Maybe Clayton wasn't so bad after all. "Enough Maxwell. I really have heard enough. If therapy is what you need, I can refer you to an excellent therapist."

"Zolla, please. This is difficult. Please..." Zolla thought she caught a glimpse of sadness in his eyes.

"Ok, but...well okay. Go ahead."

"None of that brought me peace and happiness. I never comprehended true passion or intense desire until you walked into that lobby and I laid my eyes on you. Since February the seventh, the day of our meeting, my life has been chaotic. I can't sleep at night and my concentration is off balance. I haven't been as sharp in the courtroom. Woman, you have shaken me to my core. I can't ever recall feeling this way. Zolla, you have somehow managed to awaken something I never knew existed. Earlier you asked why am I here. Well, I'm here to inform you that I'm not going anywhere. I love you. I want you and I need you in my life."

Zolla felt every nerve in her body quivering. She was stunned and found difficulty composing her thoughts. However, one thing she was certain of was that she needed to put an end to Maxwell's delusional thinking and send him on his way.

"Maxwell, I apologize if my actions towards you have been somehow misguided. You have to understand that I am a married woman, a happily married woman."

He studied her face thoroughly for a moment. He needed assurance. "No you're not." he blurted.

Zolla closed her eyes and gritted her teeth as heated blood raced through her veins like molten lava. "I beg your pardon. I can't believe you have the audacity to sit here in my office and assess my marriage. Have you loss your damn mind??"

"Oh, you heard me. I stand firm in my belief when I say that these feelings of love are mutual. I see it in your eyes. As I stand here, looking directly into your beautiful eyes,

I can feel the desire you have for me. You can maintain your false sense of reality, but I refuse to live in denial. I'm a realist, unequivocally. Shit, at this very moment, the only thing restraining me from removing all your clothes and spending the remainder of this day making love to you is God."

Zolla gasped. "Maxwell, did you here me? I'm married."

"Matter of semantics."

"Semantics? Did you say semantics? No, Maxwell it's not semantics but my reality, and yours."

"Come on, you and I both know that he is not the one. And I'm not here to play games with you. I'm a grown ass man, a big boy and you need to understand my position. It took me thirty-eight years to find you; I'm not walking away I will not let you go. Do you even comprehend how I've been affected by you? Shit, I'm in a state of conscious unconsciousness, a point of no return." He smiled. "You got me baby and you got me good. Come here. Come on over to me," he said as he removed his designer blazer and walked toward her, reaching for her hand. She hesitated but for some unexplainable reason she obliged. While looking into his penetrating stare, he took her into his arms and they both slowly exhaled as his husky whisper reached out to her.

"Do you feel that, baby? That's my heart. You got me. This is real."

Zolla was overcome with feelings of guilt and shame because at that very moment she was about to betray God, Nia, Clayton and her values. There in his arms, at that very moment, she had come to accept every emotion he felt for her. As damaging as it was for her relationship with God, it was real. She told herself that God knew her heart and she knew that there was no conning him. Maxwell held her in his arms for what seemed like an eternity. He only released her to seek refuge in her luscious lips. Slowly he brought her lips to his and she responded to him with an internal craving that matched his. Maxwell desperately tried to contain his desire but he couldn't. He carefully unbuttoned her light blue silk blouse, exposing the beautiful black laced bra that contained her ample breasts. Maxwell was caught in her rapture. He kept telling her how beautiful she was. Although his heart was racing, he kissed her neck lightly, several times. Zolla's previously stiff body now fell weak. Maxwell reached for her bra and attempted to release the hooks that kept it together. Zolla was overwhelmed with desire, but faintly heard Nia's warning and quickly urged Maxwell to stop.

"Stop! Maxwell stop. I'm married." She huffed. Maxwell reluctantly complied with her demand. He carefully buttoned her blouse and used his shoulders and arms to comfort her.

"Zolla, don't cry," he stated passionately as his shirt became soaked with her tears. "Sweetheart, you can't deny what we feel. What's your husband's name?"

She faintly remembered. "Clayton. Yes, his name is Clayton."

"Tonight you go home and tell Clayton Ramsey that it's over..."

Zolla was shocked. "You want me to do what? Have you lost your mind?"

"I love you. Zolla, I'm in love with you and you cannot deny your feelings for me. So tonight you go home and tell Mr. Ramsey that the charade is over. Tell him that there has been a change in venue. You know I'm a man with far too little patience. Therefore, it is my expectation that you accommodate my wishes so that I can spend the rest of my life accommodating yours."

With that Maxwell gave her a gentle kiss on the forehead, gathered his belongings and exited her office.

Tears fell from Zolla's eyes as she tried to make sense of all that had taken place between she and Maxwell. Her accelerated descent to despair, shame and guilt was interrupted by the ringing of her cell phone.

"Hello?"

"Heffa, where are you?"

Zolla exploded. "Leena, how many times have I told you not to refer to me as a heffa?"

"Girl, please. I've been calling you heffa ever since junior high school. What the hell is your problem? I'm only calling because the girls and I have been waiting for over an hour."

"The girls?"

"Yes, me, Nia, Fayanna, Tamera, Sherrita and Julie." There was a pregnant pause. "Oh, how could you forget your girl's birthday?"

Zolla was furious with herself. That unexpected encounter with Maxwell had her mind jumbled. As a result, she had forgotten all about the dinner party to celebrate Leena's birthday.

"Oh, Leena, I promise to make this up to you." Zolla broke down and cried.

"Listen, girl I'm worried about you. Is everything okay?" Leena was the one person who really knew Zolla and lying to her was impossible.

"No, Leena, it's not."

"Is Clayton fuckin' with you? Nia told me about the shit he's been putting you through."

"I know, Leena. I told Nia to keep you informed. But today it's not him."

"Okay, good. But you don't sound good. Can you drive safely?"

"Yes."

"Because I can come to you. This is one of my many celebrations. I celebrate my birthday the entire month."

"No Leena, it's just a hectic day. I just need to get home and rest. I just have a lot on my mind to process, important decisions to make."

"Decisions? Okay, for real. I'm worried."

"Don't Leena. Listen, we can meet tomorrow. I'm taking the day off."

"Okay, why don't we meet at Grant Park around 1 o'clock? We can walk and talk, just like old times." Zolla smiled, remembering just how much she had always enjoyed sharing precious walks around Grant Park with Leena.

"Just like old times. Okay, Leena, I'll see you mannãana."

"Girl, you are killing me with this Spanish shit."

"Bye, Leena."

"Bye, heffa."

Chapter 8

"Fuck ka Man"

It had been a while since Zolla's last visit to Grant Park. It was a popular tourist attraction and well-known for its outdoor poetry readings, concerts, art exhibits and of course its annual hosting of Chicago's very renowned "Taste of Chicago." The park was very green and lush and beyond its horizon magnificent blue water entertained an array of boats and yachts. Overweight geese, ducks and pigeons roamed the premises, being fed by the parks generous visitors. All appeared to ignore the "Please Do Not Feed the Wildlife" signs abundantly displayed.

Leena and Zolla had been at the park for over two hours. They came for exercise, but they both had consumed a slew of snacks from corn dogs and chili cheese fries to caramel corn and Zolla's favorite, ginger ale. After indulging in all the junk food, they sat and discussed their most pressing topic: Maxwell Garrison. Nia had of course told Leena all about him, which was just fine with Zolla. There were very few secrets between the three women. Leena had always liked Clayton and typically leaned in his favor if he and Zolla had a disagreement. But after hearing all of the accounts of Clayton's recent behavior, her patience had grown thin.

"Fuck Clayton! Zolla, I'm sick of his shit. What is his damn problem? He needs to pull his head out of his ass or he's going to lose you. I'm not trying to push you towards Maxwell. . . well, maybe I am."

"Leena, look, I need to be strong and look at the big picture."

"And if I'm not mistaken, that's what you've been doing for the past several months. Zolla, I just feel that life is too short and from what you've said, Clayton has emotionally checked out of your marriage and refuses all attempts by you to make the shit right."

"I know, girl. You're right."

Leena continued ranting. "Now, I'm not saying go out and have a sex fest, but, I do believe that all women, regardless of race, color or creed, should have a substitute dick on the side." Leena calmly stated while flashing a sexy half grin.

Zolla's jaw dropped. She could not believe what she was hearing.

"Wait a minute," Zolla said. "It sounds to me like you're promoting adultery."

"No, not necessarily. It's all in how you look at the situation. I choose to view it from a man's perspective."

"Here we go." Zolla rolled her eyes. "And what do you know about a man's perspective?"

"Don't be challenging me. I know the game, Leena replied with her hand on her hip. "You see, when a wife is pissed at her man and has emotionally checked out, she usually puts her coochie on lock down until further notice. Most men will make a call to the lock down temp agency."

Zolla was confused. "Lock down temp agency? Leena, what the heck are you talking about?"

"Girl, his black book."

Zolla shook her head in amazement. Leena's imagination continued to intrigue her. "Now you know not all men are like that."

"Heffa, I said most. Most is not all! Now women need to become more hip to that shit. It's really quite liberating." Leena's moment of sexual liberation was momentarily interrupted by the vigorous calling of her name.

"Leena! Leena! Hey Leena !"

"Damn, it's Jeffery Monroe and he's jogging this way. Every time I come here, I run into his baby mama drama ass."

Jeffery and Leena had dated briefly and the decision to part ways had been hers. By far she was the most fascinating woman he had ever met and reclaiming her was his goal. Leena loved the serenity long walks provided and Jeffery knew that she visited Grant Park on Wednesday and Saturday around 5:00 p.m. So he altered his jogging schedule to coincide with hers.

"What's up, Ms. Leena? It's been a long time." Leena was not in the mood for Jeffery and his bag of issues, not today.

"It's only been a week."

"Well, baby, it feels like an eternity to me." He smiled as he smacked his lips. "Girl, you look delicious in those green sweat pants and that pink halter." Leena knew he was right, she did look damn good. But she was not interested in his tired game.

"Is that right, Jeffery?" Leena asked, faking interest. "Well you know us pretty girls rock the pink and green."

"Yeah, I'm still waiting for you to return my calls. I called you every day last week, plus I left two messages for you yesterday. What's up? Your cell must be broke. I know we had good chemistry." He emphasized, "Yes indeed."

"Jeffery Monroe, the only thing that was good between us was sex."

Jeffery closed his eyes and smiled as he slowly recalled how good it was. "And baby, I miss every inch of your curvaceous body."

Zolla could not believe this conversation was taking place in front of her. She saw Leena take a deep breath. She obviously had had enough and was going to set this dude straight.

"Listen Jeffery, you're a good brotha, but like I told you months ago, I can't deal with your baby mama drama. I mean, damn Jeffery, you have six children with six different women and you always have conflict with all of them. I can't handle it. That's absolutely too much drama for me."

"I hear you, Leena. It wasn't fair to put you in the middle of all my drama. But check it out, when I get my life in order, I'm coming back for you." Leena didn't want him coming back for shit.

"Bye Jeffery, and please do not call me until the madness has stopped. I told you when we first met that pussy does not respond well to stress." Jeffery laughed heartily.

Zolla was simply speechless.

"Baby, that's why I'm crazy about you. You add spice and fun to my life. There's never a dull moment with you. You're my baby."

While jogging away he yelled, "Leena, I'll give you a call tomorrow."

"Leena, how did you ever end up with him? He definitely doesn't appear to be your type."

"And what exactly is my type?"

"I'm not quite sure but I have an idea."

"Well, to answer your question about Jeffery, I simply did the math. . . the formula." Zolla had a look of bewilderment on her face. How had she missed the formula?

"There's a formula?"

"Zolla, there's many formulas. Hell, men have theirs. When I met Jeffery I gave his looks a five, his personality a six; and his dick, I rated it a twenty. Girl, I did the math and baby girl, that man topped the charts."

Zolla's laughter brought her to tears. "Girl, you are too much, too much for me."

"What? They rate us. Why can't we play that shit too? And to answer your question about my type, heffa, you should know. You have been my friend for over twenty years. For your information, I like what is referred to as a Renaissance Man. That's a man who can play bones in the hood while smacking on chicken wings during lunch. Fly his plane to Massachusetts and dine with the Kennedy's for dinner and fly home and thoroughly fuck my ass all night long. Now, baby, that's my type, okay?" Zolla almost chocked on her ginger ale as Leena continued. "Now this Maxwell appears to be very interesting. He must be if he has you reevaluating your values. The brotha has my girl going in circles," she said in a singsong voice. "So, would you describe him as a Fuck ka man?"

Zolla laughed. "A what?"

"A fuck ka man." Zolla knew that she was setting herself up for one of Leena's over-the-top explanations.

"Okay, I give. What is a fuck ka man?"

"Girl, it describes the epitome of all men. You see, when a fuck ka man enters a room, explaining his credentials is not necessary."

"His credentials?"

"Yes girl, credentials. . . you know, his sex resume. Zolla, you know how some men feel the need to go on and on about how good they make love, how big and powerful their ding-a-lings are and insist that they're pleasers. Well, my dear, there's no need for a fuck ka man to explain shit. When he enters a room, his presence validates that he can turn your ass out, period." Zolla laughed so hard the tears had begun to smear her mascara.

"Leena, you never cease to amaze me. Girl, I have heard enough."

"No, seriously, let me finish. You do not to want to miss out on this vital information. I'm simply trying to heighten your sexual awareness. As I was saying, girl, it's in his eyes. He may be unaware that he even possesses such power, but women can feel it."

Zolla, sifted through her mental Rolodex to see if she had ever encountered a fuck ka man. She grinned as a picture of Maxwell popped into her head. "Leena, I'm assuming that they're all very attractive."

"Of course not, but, I'm not through schooling you. Remember last summer when I was having my downstairs bathroom remodeled?"

"Yes."

"Well, on this one night in particular I had all of my girls over for ladies night. We had a ball."

"Who was over?"

"Renee, Kay, Fay, Shay, Leonna, Brenda, Linda, Nia, Jorcell and that crazy ass Esther."

"Ms. Jenkins, why was I excluded? I love ladies night at your house."

"Don't even start with me. When I called to invite you, you said you were not in the mood. Some shit about you and Clayton having had words about him not spending time with you."

Zolla pouted and started to protest but Leena continued. "Darling, don't blame me for the good time you missed out on. Kick Clayton's ass. Anyway, like I was saying, the doorbell rung and in walks this contractor and girl, on the Richter scale he was a seven point two, but, something about him made us all go silent. I mean I could barley talk to the man."

Zolla laughed at Leena. "Girl, that's your response to any half decent man."

"No, baby girl, this situation was different. Girl, my coochie was quivering. The girls thought that he was a stripper. They started taking out dollar bills. Esther was drunk and started taking off her clothes."

"I'm not surprised. Why do you continue to give her alcohol, when you know she attends AA meetings?"

"Girl, Esther brought her own bottle, but you're right."

"Anyways, Jorcell stood on top of my new coffee table and started gyrating her hips while saying her favorite word: shit, shit, shit. Nia started quoting John 15. Girl, it pained me to bust their bubbles and tell those horny heffas that he was there for business, not pleasure. Luckily, he was cool. He appeared to be flattered but unaffected by the effect he had on every woman in my house."

"Humph. I bet."

"From the moment my eyes connected with that man my ovaries went into action mode, and when he left that is exactly what I told the girls." Leena chuckled.

"What's so funny?"

"They all gave me a high-five and said that he had the same effect on them, even Bible-toting Nia."

Zolla was hysterical. "Nia, oh my God."

"Yes, Nia. Anyway, you see the effect the contractor had? That's what I'm talking about. He's an example of a fuck ka man."

"I get it. I get it. Hey thanks for coming to the park and once again, forgive me for missing your birthday celebration. I promise to make it up to you."

"Listen, you already know that I celebrate my birthday the entire month. We still have a week left to celebrate. Zolla, I just want you to take care of yourself. I know that I bullshit a lot but on a serious note, always remember that you are my girl and I got your back. If you can't look into the mirror and be true to yourself then you're living a lie. Fuck what people say because people will always talk. I say that to validate this: if being married to Clayton no longer brings you joy and he continues to refuse to work on the issues at hand, then baby girl, cut your losses and walk. And if the road leads you to something more soothing to your soul, something a little more refreshing like the tall glass of water Maxwell seems to be, then girl I say go for it." Zolla desperately tried to contain the tears that were trying to surface. Leena always managed to touch her heart.

"Thank you again for your honesty and laughter. Let's touch bases by Sunday, okay."

As Leena walked away toward her vehicle, Zolla gazed at the fountain and decided Maxwell was definitely a fuck ka man.

Chapter 9

"No Expectations"

Her body stiffened with each plea because no excuse would ever justify his emotional absence from her and their marriage. It was Monday morning and boy was she pissed. Just one day prior had been their eighth anniversary and he had promised to make himself available for the special occasion. There was a reservation made weeks in advance at their favorite restaurant, Spencer's, and theater tickets for the "Color Purple."

It had been her hope that she and Clayton could make an attempt at recapturing a portion of what they once shared, just a little of his time would do. Her demand was small. She held no other expectations of him.

"Baby, I'm sorry," he pleaded.

"Clay, it's always about work. Why did you even bother coming home?" Her voice was low and vibrating with a hint of rage.

"Zolla," he begged. "Baby, just listen."

"Don't!" she yelled, cutting him off. "Don't give me excuses, Clayton. I waited at Spencer's and you never showed up. Apparently, I'm not even worthy of a phone call. For goodness sake, it was our anniversary. How could you not make our anniversary a priority?"

"Zolla," he began again. "I apologize."

She sighed as she searched her desk drawer for the bottle of Motrin she kept on hand. "You're not sorry, Clay. You see, sorry should have prompted you to give your wife a call. Sorry should have bought your butt home before two in the morning. The only thing sorry around here is your sorry..." She caught her words before they left her lips. "I want a husband, Clayton."

"You have one!" he yelled. "Woman, how many times do I have to say it?" She squeezed her eyes tightly to stop the tears from escaping. She was fed up with Mr. Ramsey and his excuses. The beeping from the phone indicating an incoming call provided an alibi. "Look Clayton, we can continue this conversation later. I have an urgent call."

"But, baby," he said in a much softer tone.

Click.

He was silenced, at least for the moment.

"Yes, Vivian?"

"It's him. . . Mr. Garrison. Shall I tell him that you're out?"

"No, put his call through." Momentarily Zolla heard his deep baritone voice.

"Hey you." It was different from his usual greeting.

"Good morning, Mr. Garrison," Zolla replied. There was a short pause before his sexy response.

"Now Zolla, we're beyond formalities. Please, address me as Maxwell."

"Okay, Maxwell. To what do I owe this call?"

Maxwell was cool and masterful with his choice of words. "I want to serve you."

She quickly moved the phone away from her ear to gather her racing thoughts. She was stunned she could not believe his words. "S-s-serve me?" she stammered. "You want to serve me?"

"Yes, I want to bring you to my home tonight, prepare dinner and serve you."

She knew that going to his home and being served was definitely out of the question. On his turf? No, she would never allow herself to be placed in such a position. "I'm sorry, but I don't think it's appropriate—me being in your home, alone, with you."

Deep within his soul he knew she was probably right. "Okay, I'll take you out to one of Chicago's finest restaurants."

She desperately tried to control the rumbles coming from her stomach. She was starving. "I'm not hungry," she lied.

"Okay, well I know the perfect little spot where we can go for drinks and be entertained by soft music."

"Look, Maxwell, I don't drink." Obviously taken aback by her tone, Maxwell paused.

"Zolla, you're not making this easy for me. All I want is a little selfish time with you. I promise to behave myself. Meet me at the Westin Hotel off Lake Front Drive. Do you know the location?" His body was craving her and he knew that taming his desire to make love to her would be a challenge but he had to find the self-control or he would lose her.

Zolla was furious. "Maxwell, for goodness sake! A hotel? Now, I understand. This is simply about sex. How dare you assume that I would entertain the possibility of giving myself to a man that I barely know. Have you forgotten that I'm married and that I'm a decent woman?"

"Wait, that's not my intention," he lied. "Please be assured of that. I simply selected the Westin because of the location and the hotel's lounge is magnificent. Thursday night is soft jazz. I believe tonight Kamilah Devoe and R. Nelson are both performing." Zolla loved Kamilah Devoe and R. Nelson. "We can sit by the pond under candlelight and simply talk, okay?" Zolla was not quite buying the old 'we'll just talk' routine. She needed reassurance.

"Nothing more, Maxwell? No expectations?

"Nothing more. My only expectation is that you relinquish to me time with you." Zolla could not deny that Maxwell's attentiveness was addicting.

"What time?"

"Six-thirty."

"See you at six-thirty."

"You most certainly will, Mrs. Ramsey."

Chapter 10

"A Reflection of Her Indiscretions"

As she drove up North Michigan Avenue she felt a sense of energy. As night approached the city appeared to come alive, especially The Westin Hotel. It was absolutely beautiful, one of Zolla's favorites. Its incredible architecture, brilliant colors and magnificent decor made her creative senses come alive. Zolla had a fascination for frequenting hotels and suddenly found herself longing for an overdue visit to the highest ranking hotel on her list, the Las Vegas Wynn.

Upon entering the valet, she quickly applied a light coat of bronze lipstick, touched up her foundation and secured her hair in a bun. The moment her long, shapely legs stepped out of her BMW, all eyes were on her. Although she had no idea she'd be seeing Maxwell this evening, she was glad she had worn one of her favorite outfits to work. As usual, she looked absolutely stunning in her pure white double-breasted blazer and matching skirt that was hemmed several inches above the knee. Her gold Coach stilettos accented the suit perfectly. She also happened to be wearing the diamond earrings she purchased for herself while vacationing with Leena in South Beach, Florida last summer. They added just enough bling while telling onlookers that she was indeed a class act.

Wherever Zolla ventured, men practically fell to their knees, begging for just a glimpse of acknowledgment from her. But Zolla appeared oblivious to the havoc she created. As she strolled into the hotel toward the pond, she held her head high and scanned the area. She saw several couples who appeared love struck as they listened to the smooth voice of Kamilah Devoe. At the bar, there were various people ordering drinks. Sitting at a small table in the seductiveness of candlelight was Maxwell. He was wearing a sexy smile and a look of approval.

My God, could this woman be any finer? And those big beautiful legs. . . she's unbelievable.

Maxwell had a foot fetish and when his eyes settled on her freshly pedicured feet he saw perfection.

He suddenly realized that Zolla had made it to the table and was standing directly in front of him. He stood up to pull out her chair. "Zolla, you look beautiful."

She smiled. "You don't look bad yourself. It's nice to see you dressed down for a change."

"Never underestimate me. I'm full of surprises." He winked. "I can do casual."

Zolla definitely approved as she wanted to say, *Yes, you can and you do it very, very well.* But she kept quiet. She didn't want to over inflate his already huge ego. But he did look good in his gray wool slacks, light gray cashmere turtleneck, and gray shoes. The flicker of the candlelight reflected on his silver Rolex watch. While Zolla did not usually like men with earrings, the small silver hoop that hung from his right ear was somehow sexy. Zolla's tense body felt tingles and then she was overcome with relaxation as the soothing sounds of jazz filled the room. The two of them sat and engaged in small talk.

Maxwell spotted a waiter and signaled him over to the table. "So, what would you like to drink?" he asked Zolla.

"I'll have a ginger ale with a twist of lemon."

The young waiter, who looked like a skateboarder, jotted down her request. "And for you, sir?"

"Oh, I'll have Remy Martin Louis the thirteenth." The waiter nodded and quickly left to fill the order.

Zolla could not resist the sudden urge to be mischievous. She leaned over close and said, "Ya know Maxwell, one can tell a lot about a man by what he drinks."

Maxwell smiled while staring at her lustfully. "I'm very aware of that."

Zolla surrendered. He had won the playful battle of sexual innuendos. "You are too much."

"I haven't even begun," he said with a smile. Instantly, the look on his face became serious. It was almost scary.

"What?" Zolla asked in a worried tone.

Maxwell cleared his throat before answering. "Okay, it's not my intention to make you uncomfortable, but I need to know."

"Know what?"

"Did you inform Clayton?"

"Inform Clayton of what?"

Maxwell huffed. He was obviously irritated. "Woman, did you inform him of your decision to end your marriage?" Zolla's eyes widened in complete surprise. She could not believe his audacity. "It was my expectation that you—"

"Your expectation!" Zolla raised her voice and a woman nearby looked at her, annoyed. "What do you mean by your expectation?" she whispered between gritted teeth. "Conforming to your ideologies is not my expectation. It's not my expectation at all. Let's be perfectly clear, my decision to walk away from my marriage or stay is simply that, my decision. My choice! Do you understand?"

"I just need for you to—" Once again his words were quickly silenced.

"No, Maxwell. Do you understand my words to you? She peered into his eyes and pointed her right index finger at him. "You cannot control my behavior or my life."

"Yes, but this situation is quite challenging. I feel like a mad man." And that he did. He did not know why Zolla had come into his life, and he didn't care. All he knew was that he'd fallen in love with her and under no circumstance did he plan on losing her, not to anyone or anything, ever.

Slowly leaning over, his piercing stare sealed his heart's stance. "Baby, I love you and I want you completely. I want everything you have to give." He paused to let the revelation sink in. "I'm not delusional. I know that I'm a selfish bastard and I can live with that, but losing you is not something I can do or will do."

Hearing the words "love" and "losing you" in the same breath triggered painful memories and caused Zolla to remember the story that had haunted her for the past twenty-three years. They were memories she had long ago buried and only recently shared with her two best friends. Now, she felt compelled to share them with Maxwell.

While Zolla sat with a blank stare, her thoughts were racing. How could he profess to loving her when he barely knew her? And yes, he was right about one reality, he was delusional if he thought she could ever relive her mother's indiscretions. Zolla was painfully aware of one sure way to terminate Maxwell's desires. The disclosing of her past, the secret that she sealed away, the horrible secret that was the source of years of pain and family shame. If he knew, then surely he would protect her and walk away.

Maxwell was on the brink of frustration. He finally told her how he really felt. He had never allowed himself to display such vulnerability as she sat speechless. He was about to break the silence when Zolla softly whispered, "Maxwell, I need for you to calm down and listen to what I have to say." Still uncertain of his perceptions, she cautiously continued. "Please, if you care about me as much as you claim then sit back and clear your mind as I share an intimate story with you. Can you do that for me?"

Maxwell sensed the seriousness of her words and without hesitation he complied. "Ok, sweetheart," he replied calmly.

"I want to share with you a story involving a tragic event that occurred several years ago. I'm hoping that these accounts will provide you with a clear understanding as to why I hold the values that I do and why we can only have a friendship. That's it, Maxwell, a beautiful friendship, nothing more."

Maxwell forced a smile he did not feel; as he slowly brought the glass of fine liquor to his mouth and swallowed the remainder. He didn't find pleasure in being apart of any theatrics that would tear her away from him.

Zolla took a deep breath. "My mother once told me that when she met my father it was love at first sight. They married after dating for only six months. Soon after, I was born and five years later mom was pregnant with my brother Zion. My parents had a beautiful marriage. As a kid, I thought it was perfect. As a family we did everything together. Our home was absolutely lovely. My mother was an excellent home maker and cook. Zion and I felt loved each and every day."

As focused as he was on each word departing from her lips, he couldn't help but notice the unwelcoming sadness within her eyes.

"And my father, he and I shared the most beautiful relationship." Zolla continued "He was the most important person in my life. I was his baby girl and when he spoke to me or just looked in my direction I could feel the pride he held within his heart for me. We were like peanut butter and jelly and all who witnessed our interactions knew it." Zolla lifted her head slightly and tenderly gazed into Maxwell's eyes as she carefully chose her words to reveal the most important part of the story. "My father and I had gone away to spend two weeks with my Nanna. At least once a year my family would spend two weeks with my Nanna. But that particular year my mother had been hired to make five dresses for her friend's daughter's wedding and could not get away. Zion stayed with my mother because she felt that due to his young age he should not travel without her. We always had a fabulous time in Chicago and this trip was no different. My Nanna's home was always filled with our various relatives. Each would plant kisses on my cheeks until they felt bruised.

Zolla went on talking about a large family gathering similar to *Soul Food*-like occasions that Maxwell's own family had. She described the event at length and gave details about the menu that included dishes like honey baked squash, collard greens, buttermilk fried chicken, and peach cobbler. Maxwell was starving and Zolla's illustrations only increased his appetite

"Woman, I could eat a horse right now and all that food you're talking about is torture." She joined him in a moment of laughter.

"Well, as you can see I loved my Nanna and her cooking and that's why when my father suggested that we cut our trip short it devastated me. You see, just before our trip to Chicago, he and my mother had a disagreement and he had suddenly realized his insensitivity toward her. I remember begging him to stay longer, but Daddy showed no mercy. He said, "Baby girl, some situations between adults are difficult for children to understand." With that, we were on our way back home to surprise my mother with her favorite chocolate and white roses. Once we got there, to not be detected, we parked several houses down from ours. The house was dark, but my mom's white Mercedes was parked in the driveway. My father...my father and I—"

Zolla was fighting back tears and she was getting choked up. "We just assumed that she and Zion were asleep."

Maxwell reached across the table and gently took her hands in his. "Sweetheart, don't cry. You don't have to continue. You're obviously troubled by these memories—"

"No, I have to." She interrupted. "This pain has tormented me for years. I'll be just fine. Just allow me to finish, okay?"

Maxwell gave her a supportive nod. "Ok."

"My father and I quietly entered the house. I was so excited. I just knew that my mother would be overcome with joy and then my father would be vindicated. As we both tiptoed towards their bedroom, the sounds of soft music and laughter echoed from the door. I think that my father and I both assumed that mom was listening to music while playing with Zion. We both agreed that Daddy would count to three and then open the door and that's exactly what happened." Tears flowed from her eyes as she repeated those words. "Maxwell, that's exactly what we did. Why did we do it?"

"Zolla, what did you see?" he carefully questioned.

"The door flew open. I closed my eyes and enthusiastically yelled surprise! And when I opened my eyes I saw my mother on the bed, naked, and this man was lying between her legs. I was frozen. In one fell swoop, my father screamed and ran over to the bed. He grabbed that man by the neck and began choking him. My mother was screaming, crying; and begging for my father to stop. I can remember my father yelling 'I'm gonna kill this bastard. I'm gonna kill him and then, Narvella, I'm gonna kill you.' My mother grabbed a blanket and dashed out of the house and over to our neighbor's to call the police. I grabbed my father by his waist and pleaded for him to just stop. Maxwell, I pleaded and pulled and pleaded some more. Finally, my father released him. Both men fell to the floor, but the other man was gasping for air. My father looked up at me and cried. Eventually the police came and they handcuffed Daddy and drug him from our home like a criminal.

Outside, nosy neighbors were aware that something very disturbing had taken place at our house. My mom was standing on the lawn with a blue blanket to conceal her nude body from watchful eyes. As my father was drug past her, he was yelling, 'Narvella, how could you do this to our family? If I see him again I'm rippin' his head off! You tell him that. Tell your lover that!' As my father approached where I was standing, he looked into my eyes. I saw hopelessness, shame and despair. Embarrassed, my mother ran into the house. Later I found her on the kitchen floor, naked and crying. I was overcome with intense anger and fear. I started yelling and told her that I hated her and that she would never be forgiven.

Several days later my father physically returned home, but emotionally he was destroyed. I believe that my mother's infidelity hurt him to his core, destroyed his spirit. Immediately, I knew that my life, my childhood, would be forever transformed. As time went on, my parents tried to recapture what they'd had but Daddy could never forgive my mother. I found solace in continuously blaming her for destroying our family. She had betrayed my father and as a result, one day he left for work and never returned." Zolla closed her eyes and bit down on her lower lip before continuing. Kamilah's smooth voice had a calming effect, lessening Zolla's anxiety as she continued. "He simply walked away from his life as a parent, a provider and a spouse. But most of all, because of my mother's selfishness, my father walked out of my life."

"Zolla, how's your relationship with your parents now?"

"Well, when my father walked out, he never looked back. I don't know whether he's dead or alive. I last saw him when I was twelve years old. As for my mother, our relationship continues to be strained."

Maxwell was blown away by Zolla's story but felt a sense of pride that she chose him to share it with. He shook his head. "Wow, Zolla, it's very disappointing hearing that."

"You're right. And what's even more disappointing is that two years after my father walked away, I left Fiji to live with my Nanna in Chicago. I had become so rebellious toward my mother that she could no longer control me. I would speak to her on a regular basis while in Chicago but I had no desire to see her."

"But, no matter what she has done, she's still your mother and I'm sure she loves you."

Zolla shrugged her shoulders. "Well, now I hope that you can understand my issues with infidelity. I've seen what deceit and selfishness can do to a marriage. I don't want to be a reflection of my mother's indiscretions."

"You won't be. I don't know your mother but I know a little about you. I know that seated before me is a beautiful woman with a caring nature," he said as he reached across the table and lifted her chin. "Yes, your mother made a poor choice but you cannot continue to judge her. Her indiscretions continue to have profound effects on you." At that moment, the waiter came by to offer refills on their drinks but seeing the intense look on Maxwell's face, he kept walking to the next table. "Sweetheart," Maxwell went on, "I refuse to cheapen what I feel for you to an indiscretion. In the words of the great philosopher; Mike Tyson, "That's ludicrous!" Zolla matched his dimpled smiled. "Listen, go away with me this weekend. I own a small cottage in Wisconsin. You'll love it."

Zolla could not believe him. Had he not heard one word she had shared with him?

"Are you serious?" Zolla asked incredulously. "For the past two hours I opened my soul to you. Do you even comprehend how I've been impacted by everything I've shared with you?"

"Yes Zolla, of course. I empathize with you. But as I stated earlier, you're not your mother. I simply want to take you away. We can even sleep in separate rooms. I won't even touch you. Sweetheart, I want isolation with you." Zolla was perplexed once again. His words had filled her with amazement. *Isolation? Did he just say that he wanted isolation with me?*

She inhaled and released slowly. "Maxwell, I can't. Yes, I have feelings for you. I really do. But our timing is off. Maybe years ago, if I would have taken a different course in life, our paths would have crossed. I just don't know. I can't have everything that my soul desires. I can't." Maxwell knew that he was grasping at straws as feelings of desperation reared their ugly head. Without saying a word, he removed a business card from his wallet and wrote information on the back of it.

"Ok, this is my address. If you should have a decline in guilt, I will be departing tomorrow at noon, okay?"

Zolla eyes rested on the business card as she gently ran a hand over her hair and down the nape of her neck. She massaged her neck and shoulders to alleviate the stiffness. All of her tension and frustration settled in that region. He didn't miss the expression of frustration that crossed her face as he pulled two crisp one-hundred dollar bills out of his wallet to settle the bill as she pleaded with him. "Maxwell."

She argued softly. "I have a husband at home. What about Clayton? Have you thought about him?"

Maxwell gave her a penetrating stare as he pushed back his chair, stood and proceeded to slowly walk away and without the aid of a backward glance, his riveting words drove through her soul. "Clayton, baby you're worried about Clayton? Fuck Clayton! He had his chance and he blew it." Before exiting the lounge he turned and asked as she sat motionless, "Zolla, what about me?"

Chapter 11

"Balls of Confusion"

I t was extremely late and her naked body awaited his arrival. She could not believe just how freely she was giving herself to a man she could barely identify. But he was hungry for her, and she had a sexual craving that needed to be tamed, even though her gut feeling was that the upcoming event wasn't quite right. But hell, the swelling and intense throbbing between her legs indicated that this was something very much necessary.

She entered the room and slowly glided toward the bed as the moonlight's seductive shadow covered every inch of his naked body. His words flowed like warm honey as her anxious body responded to each syllable.

"Shit, I'm about to explode," he said. "Tonight your body will be my private buffet, an-all-I-can-eat buffet, and I'm coming back for several helpings." Her body trembled as a chill surged up her spine. "Do you understand the magnitude of this situation? No zone will be left unexplored, not tonight, baby. Are you ready?"

She nodded yes, as she slowly closed her almond-shaped eyes while planting delicate kisses on his bald head. He was extremely skilled and tonight his sexual desire had reached its full capacity as nearly an hour was spent massaging her entire body. He started with her delicate feet, placing each toe into his mouth. A warm Jasmine oil was used to help bring her tensed body to complete calm. In the midst of her tranquility, he spread her legs and feasted on her most intimate spot. Her fingernails sank deep into the tight muscles of his shoulders as she tried suppressing the uncontrollable raw savage screams as his hands cradled her butt, pulling her closer and closer for what felt like an eternity, leaving her grasping for her sanity.

"Are you okay, baby?" he asked ever so softly, knowing the power he had.

She couldn't speak. Instead, tears flowed from her eyes, giving validation that part one of his mission had been accomplished. And when their bodies finally joined, she cried out, not in pain but in appreciation—appreciation that he had come to her on this wondrous night and touched her heart and soul. There she lay on white satin sheets in front of a luminous fireplace, making passionate love to this wonderful man, pulling and grasping every inch of him into her. She took every bit of his hardness as it slid in and out with a force so powerful, she trembled in her struggle to find her breath. She surrendered to him the solitude he had craved. In her womb, he felt her very essence. Their bodies, like the ocean, ebbed and flowed in complete unison. His breathing was hard and ragged. Their bodies were drenched in sweat as he held on for dear life and released every drop of his being into her pulsating body. Her eyes remained shut as she accepted the reality that this was not a mistake and there would be no regrets.

He released her tenderly and turned over to indulge in rest. He couldn't remember the last time he had such a powerful orgasm. After that, plus the several trips to Zolla's buffet, he was in desperate need of physical rejuvenation, but not before his words of gratitude reached out to her.

"Good night, baby. I don't know what got into you tonight. All I can say is damn."

Zolla opened her eyes and turned to give him a gentle kiss on his right cheek. "Oh my God!" she gasped. Her eyes widened.

He smiled coyly, proud of his performance. He had indeed spent the last couple hours having the best sex he had ever experienced. But the look on Zolla's face was one of utter shock and the look on his was one of confusion. "What's wrong, baby? You look as though you've just seen a ghost?"

Zolla thought of how for once Clayton was right on the money. Unbeknownst to him, in the height of her mental delusion, she had subconsciously bedded the wrong pair of balls.

Chapter 12

"Just Trying to Get to Heaven"

Zolla was overcome with conscious thoughts securely nestled in a cloud of mounting guilt, undeniable guilt. It was 10:00 a.m. the following morning as she sat on the terrace of her backyard overlooking the sprawling acreage. Acres draped by an expanse of lush emerald green and several cherry blossom trees. To her left sat a picturesque flower garden.

Zolla was surrounded by elegance and tranquility and at the moment she was held hostage in a grand oasis of evergreens, flowers and water. Her captives were insistent that her desires be thoroughly entertained. The irises, white daffodils and purple violets opened their delicate petals toward the heavens, as the pink, red, white and yellow roses stood tall and poised; competing for Zolla's approval.

Directly in front of the patio was a large oval pool elevated four feet above the terrace. Several earth-toned slated stairs granted access to its glistening waters. Zolla loved how the water appeared to cascade over its edge. The pool's most entertaining feature was the attached bar and Jacuzzi. A small red brick guest house was perfectly positioned forty feet to the right of the pool. Zolla recalled how she had pleaded with Clayton to insist that the gardeners construct a small lake next to their guest house and have it filled with koi. The request had been made several years prior and the koi had matured in size. Yes, visually the grounds of the Ramsey estate were a paradise.

However, the imagery alone was not powerful enough to derail her conflictive thoughts. *What's going on with me? What in the hell am I doing? Why is this man in my thoughts; in my bed?* She tried to conceal her tear-soaked face with both hands as her words revealed the simple truth. *I just need to be honest with myself. Ever since I laid eyes on him I've felt something. I feel as though our meeting was predestined but how can that be when there's Clay? Yet, every day, every minute, each and every second I find myself craving him, longing to see him. I can't help it. I know God is going to be pissed with me."* In her heart Zolla knew that God had already surpassed her inclination. She was caught up and twisted in this rapture of confusion and hypocrisy. *I need insight. I need someone to help me save myself."* Zolla sighed. She knew what had to be done, where to gather the needed insight. Yes, she knew but she was too guilt ridden to face God. She gave a heavy sigh as she watched four blue jays compete for an Artist-of-the-Year Grammy.

Instantly, Zolla concluded that she was in desperate need of a vacation. After a call to Rigo, her travel agent, weeks later, she Nia and Leena were basking in the sun near an Olympic size pool in Cancun, Mexico. Each woman sported a fashionable florescent bikini. Nia's was aqua, Zolla's tangerine and Leena's a lemon lime.

A handsome young waiter eagerly approached the three beauties, delighted to be of services to them.

"Senorita, what will you be having today?" he asked.

"Baby, I'll have an apple martini." The fact that Leena called him baby put a huge smile on his deeply tanned face. He then turned his attention to Zolla.

"Y tu lindo, te gustaria?"

"Me gustaria una Jamaica por favor."

"Algo mas?"

"No, gracias."

"God damn Zolla, why couldn't you just say punch? You're making us all look bad!"

"Oh, I'm sorry Ms. Leena. I just believe that when in Rome do as the Romans," she smiled. "By the way, jealously isn't becoming of you."

The waiter turned to Nia. "And you senorita?"

"Well," she paused, straining to read his name tag. "Fredrico, I'll have a grande black ice tea, lightly sweetened, with two pumps instead of four. Please make sure that you use two pumps. And did I mention nine ice cubes? Not seven, eight, or ten. Yesterday Ricardo was bartending and he gave me eight. Thank you, Fredrico."

Leena was shocked. For the sake of all liberated women, she had to say something. "See, that's why your frigid ass needs a man. If you had nine inches of dick nestled in your coochie, you would not be worried about nine fuckin' ice cubes."

Zolla batted her eyes rapidly, embarrassed by Leena's poor choice of words. *Had she not noticed the two older couples sun bathing close by?* "Leena Jenkins, watch your mouth," Zolla said between gritted teeth.

Chuckling softly, Leena rested her right hand on her butt cheek as she pointed it in Zolla's direction. "Kiss my big sexy ass, Zolla."

"Bring it over here and I will."

Leena did a double take, and stood shocked with her mouth wide open.

Zolla shrugged her shoulders. "Well, after all these years of friendship, I guess you're finally rubbing off on me Ms. Sassy Frazee.

"Hush you two. And Leena, for your information I have met a very interesting young man." Leena and Zolla looked back at each other and jumped up and down with excitement and started dancing.

Nia just shook her head. "You two are out of your minds."

"No, baby girl, this is called being happy for your girl. Now give us the 411."

"Okay, Zolla do you remember our conversation at Magnolia's when I explained to you how the spirit had moved me to pray for you?"

Zolla smiled, nodding. "Of course I do."

"While at the pulpit praying with Pastor Aggie, I felt someone grab my hand. I just automatically assumed that it was sister Mary J. Walker, Brother Al or Deacon Smith, but when I opened my eyes I saw this gorgeous, tall hunk of deliciousness. He had the most amazing smile and before I could even blink, he embraced me and whispered into my ear, 'Your friend is going to be just fine. God has already taken care of her situation.'"

"Nia, you've been keeping this man a secret for all these months? Girl, shame on you." Zolla said in mock anger.

'No, after our encounter at church several months ago our paths did not cross again until last last month at Pastor Aggies's Annual Singles Retreat. He approached me and asked if my prayers for you had been answered."

"Okay, wait a minute. Are you confessing to sharing my marital problems with our entire congregation?"

"Of course not. Please don't insult my loyalty. You already knew that God was in control of that entire situation. Reese, that's his name, caught me by surprise when he admitted to praying that our paths would cross. And I nearly fainted because I had prayed that same prayer. From that moment on we became inseparable."

"Well shit, what does Reese do?"

"What do you mean by 'do' Leena?"

"As in what does he do to pay his damn bills?"

"Well, if you must know, he's the assistant dean over at the School of Public Health at the University of Michigan and he's also a published author. He writes under an alias. After our third date he invited me to a book signing."

Leena and Zolla both loved reading and were very much intrigued. "Whose book signing? They asked in unison.

"His. Can you believe it? Leena, as a matter of fact, you have several of his books. He writes under an alias."

Leena could not contain her growing curiosity. "Is he Edwin Brown?"

"No."

"Xavier Richardson?"

"Nope."

"R. D. Jacobson?"

"Not even close."

"Oh, I know. Deonte Moore?"

"No, no, no, Leena, I can't reveal his identity. I made a promise to him. That's the purpose of writing under an alias. He wants to be anonymous."

"Well you probably have me mixed up with Zolla anyway. I own very few Christian books."

"Leena, trust me, his books are on your shelf. They're about love, faith and passion. Although, he is a faithful man of God and he was sent to me. Hallelujah." Nia threw her hands in the air toward heaven.

Zolla laughed at Nia's excitement. "So girl, did you ever ask why he grabbed your hand at church?"

"You best believe I did."

"And what did he say?"

"He looked directly into my eyes and said that God led him to me, and he felt that no further explanation was needed."

It was 5:00 p.m. and the evening entertainment, an energetic Cuban band had taken center stage and Ms. Jenkins was feeling the fire as she stood and flung her lime green wrap onto her poolside chaise lounge and proceeded to entertain the crowd with that addicting wiggle.

"This band is the shit! Ya'll gon' make me lose my mind up in here, up in here," she chanted as she wiggled her hips in Nia's direction. "Anyway girl, that's my kind of man. Does he have any brothers, cousins, uncles? A divorced father or a great grand daddy?" Nia rolled her eyes as she stood to hug the poolside entertainment. No, not the Cuban band but Leena.

"Hush, Leena!" Nia said and then turned to Zolla. "I don't want to prematurely claim this man but I just feel that he is the one." Leena's hips took a short intermission from entertaining the crowd as she switched to the lounge and took a sip of her apple martini.

"Well Nia, you're not the only one with juicy news to report. Quincy had two dozen pink roses sent to me," Leena announced.

Zolla wasn't surprised to hear Quincy's name. She had met him several years ago at one of Leena's company functions. Leena was a columnist for a local woman's health magazine. In recent years the magazine had flourished and was bestowed many awards. The Editor in Chief was very much impressed with Leena's creative insight and had given her significant creative latitude. Out of gratitude the publisher paid tribute to the entire staff with a dinner and dance at the downtown Hilton. At that event, Quincy's attentiveness and interest in Leena was obvious.

"Quincy? The brother from the magazine, the photographer?" Nia inquired.

"Ain't that a bitch? Took me out to lunch two weeks ago and told me that he's been attracted to me since he started at the magazine two years ago." Leena put her hand on her hip and asked, "Zolla, why are you smiling?"

"Because he's a good guy. He's handsome, intelligent, a good sense of humor and he appears to care about you. I always thought that the two of you would be good together."

Zolla liked Quincy. She appreciated that he adored Leena. Leena had hosted many suitors but Quincy held a special spot in Leena's heart because he was sweet and Zolla could see that.

"Well, I don't know about all of that. But Zolla, he's seen all of my trueness: My intellectual side, my lady of society persona, my sex kitten/wannabe exotic dancer side, my ghetto fabulous put-yo-ass-in check persona, as well as the compassionate side of me. And he is smitten with the entire package. And that's exactly what he conveyed to me last week over dinner."

Zolla and Nia gave each other a high five. "Girl, we are scared of you."

"No, baby girls, be scared for him. You know I'm a handful." Zolla knew that Leena was a challenge, but she was also a blessing to all that knew her.

"Yes, but Leena you're also exceptionally smart, honest, compassionate, loyal, funny and you have a big beautiful heart." All three friends found difficulty in containing their tears.

"Zolla?"

"Yes, Nia?"

"Thanks for sharing your story with Leena and I. When I opened your letter and read it, girl I cried. Reading the accounts of your childhood actually brought tears to my eyes."

"Nia, I didn't mean to bring you to tears but writing that letter was therapy. That pen and paper helped me to connect with multiple layers of buried pain."

"Z, please don't misunderstand me. My tears were tears of gratitude. I was grateful that God helped you to find much-needed peace and closure. You had been carrying around your mother's pain for over twenty years, blaming yourself for what you perceived as her indiscretions."

"Girl, you had me boo-hooing too."

"Tears! You, Leena?"

"Yes, Me! I never truly understood all the shit you endured until I read your letter. Girl, you have to make peace with your mother. Yes, she messed up, but if we are blessed to live long enough, we are all going to experience our share of fuck-ups. Baby, that's Life 101. She's human and you can't continue to hold her to some unrealistic expectation."

"What unrealistic expectation?" Zolla questioned.

"Your expectation of what being human represents. Just live a little longer Zolla and you will find yourself confronted with some unimaginable situations that will have you on your knees."

Nia raised her hand toward the sky and said, "Amen, amen and amen."

Leena continued, "The truth is, life can do that to you, to all of us. None of us are perfect. We are all, for the most part, just trying to get to heaven. Even the most dysfunctional person is just trying to get to heaven. There are very few people who just don't give a damn. Many just get lost because their lives are consumed with unnecessary bullshit."

"I know that you and Nia are right. Writing that letter was equivalent to a physical and emotional healing. For twenty-three years, I have been carrying around unnecessary baggage and pain. The pain of my mother's disgrace, pain of my father's shame, and the pain of a fragmented childhood. And yes, I have been extremely intolerant and judgmental. I believe that was my subconscious way of not identifying with my mother's infidelity. I projected all of my pain on all of those who, from my perspective, identified with her indiscretion. You know, like Connie, Phyllis, Gabriella and the list goes on, and on. I was wrong. I had no right to be so extreme. And yes, life does have a way of humbling you and forcing you to look at your own stuff. I do believe that's what growth is all about. Nia and Leena nodded their heads in agreement. "Over the past several months I have made a tremendous amount of growth and recently I have made some serious decisions."

Leena looked surprised. "What decisions? Is this in regards to Maxwell and Clayton?"

"I really can't say at this time but what I will say to you is that I'm at peace with this process. I'm at peace with myself."

After Leena and Nia had settled into their suites for the night, Zolla returned to her seventh floor suite and stood on her balcony, taking in all that was magnificent. Her eyes settled on the blanket of sparkling blue sprawled before her. Yes, she was in a good place. Emotionally, Zolla felt better than she had in a long time. Upon returning home she would ensure that her life was a reflection of all that brought her a sense of peace. There was simply no turning back.

Chapter 13

"Suite 2026"

As Maxwell's meeting with Lloyd concluded his mind was miles away. He missed everything about Zolla. It seemed like years since his eyes were last entranced by her beauty. Actually it had only been several weeks since they last shared a conversation. She was the one who decided to put some distance between the two of them. But Maxwell continued leaving messages and sending flowers. He had even purchased ruby earrings and had them delivered to her office by courier, his feeble attempt to remain in her thoughts.

He was taken by surprise when he heard a message she left on his voice mail. He was even more perplexed when she asked him to meet her later that evening at the Hyatt Hotel. He had been summoned to promptly arrive at eight p.m. and to phone her cell for further instruction once he was in the hotel lobby.

Consumed with anxiousness, Maxwell's thoughts intensified. *Mrs. Ramsey, woman what are you up to? This definitely is out of your character.* Maxwell couldn't help but recall his last meeting with Zolla at a hotel and how she had gone ballistic, accusing him of plotting. He sighed. "Oh, Mrs. Ramsey, you got me going in circles."

Hours later he glanced at his Patek Phillppe, which revealed it was time, time to go to her, the woman he loved, to face his possible crucifixion. A shiver of apprehension swept his spine but he quickly dismissed it as he entered, the Hyatt Hotel, sat down in a large brown leather chair, took a minute to collect his thoughts and then did as he had been instructed.

Her instructions were short and precise. "Come to suite 2026."

The elevator ride to the twentieth floor felt like the longest ride of his life and when Zolla opened the door of the presidential suite, she took his breath away. In the past, many women had tried, but until Zolla none had been successful. She stood before him wearing a cranberry silk teddy. It appeared to have been tailored to fit every inch of her curvaceous body. Her hair was secured in a neat bun. Her lips were covered with a cranberry lipstick and she was wearing the ruby earrings he had sent to her. Maxwell, in all his years, had never laid eyes on anything more beautiful or sensual. He stepped into the suite, smiling with arms opened. She came to him with ease and slowly brought her lips to his. Damn, he wanted her. He had to have her, but he did not want to assume anything. Assuming could lead to a catastrophe, so he remained cautious. Slowly he walked into the ambiance of earth tones, brown, beige, splashes of coral and a hint of pale blue, harmonizing gently with walls painted in a custom white botanical chinoiserie pattern. The living room was dominated by an invasive nineteenth century bronze and crystal chandelier. In the center of the octagonal living room sat two identical custom sofas uphol-stered in white linen and decorated with several chocolate and gold velvet pillows. The sofas sat facing each other and were separated by a massive Victorian cherry wood coffee table.

To the far right of the sofas sat two large Louis XVI wing chairs covered in chocolate cannele silk. Each chair was decorated with two soft pillows that were accented with a mixture of bronze silk and pale blue antique French embroidery. Behind the two elegant chairs stood four massive French doors leading out to a terrace overlooking the city.

The Presidential suite's most impressive feature was its winding staircase leading to its master bedroom. Opposite the foyer a lit fire place provided soothing warmth, an appetizer to Maxwell's senses and an invitation to the unknown.

"Sweetheart," he said softly, "why was I summoned here?" he asked, stressing every syllable.

"Maxwell, let's sit by the fireplace," Zolla said as she reached for his hand and steered him into the living room. He gave her a skeptical look.

Zolla held his gaze as she nestled her body between his legs. She took a deep breath before speaking. "I just returned from vacationing in Mexico, and while there I made some decisions, very important decisions. I brought you here, Mr. Garrison, to tell you that I believe that I fell in love with you the moment I laid my eyes on you." She closed her eyes and recalled when she saw the back of his head in her office. Since that day she thought of him daily. As much as she tried to ignore the feelings, she couldn't. She even thought of him as she had sex with her husband. "You are my soul mate and I can no longer deny it. It is what it is." Zolla tenderly placed her hands on his face. "It is what it is and tonight I want to make love to you. I want you to lose your essence in the womb of a woman who loves you completely."

Maxwell was a warrior who was seldom brought to tears. In fact, the last time he could recall shedding tears was at his mother's funeral twenty-five years ago. But there in her arms, in the secrecy and ambience of suite 2026, tears flowed from his eyes as his lover skillfully undressed him, removing his blazer, tie, and shirt. Within moments his belt, pants, underwear, socks and shoes were in a pile on the floor. He sat in the silence of suite 2026 as his soul mate passionately kissed him and thanked him for coming into her life.

Zolla's heart began to race and her lips trembled. She smiled up at him, batted her long lashes and as she leaned closer, her lips pressed against his smooth brown skin. "Maxwell, make love to me," she said, barely above a whisper. "Baby, please make love to me."

Maxwell eagerly removed her camisole and could not believe his eyes. Her body was perfect, absolutely amazing. He gently laid her on the Oriental rug.

"Sweetheart, are you okay?"

"Yes, I…I just don't want to get pregnant."

Maxwell froze. He did not come prepared. "I had no idea we'd be making love."

Zolla did. It had been her intention and she had come prepared. "No problem. Can you hand me my purse?" She dug into the side pocket of her designer handbag and pulled out a foil-wrapped packet. "Here. I knew that there could be a possibility." She winked.

Observing Maxwell as he secured his manhood made her nervous. Mr. Garrison was well equipped and she silently prayed her body could accommodate him. "Maxwell, I'm nervous."

"Sweetheart, I promise to be gentle. I love you. I'll go slowly, okay?"

"Thank you." She replied.

"Sweetheart, you are my blessing and I love you. Do you hear me? I love you." Starting with the top of her head, Maxwell kissed every inch of her body. His touch drove her insane, and when he took hostage of her 36 D's, Zolla had simultaneous orgasms. She had never experienced such fulfillment. It wasn't so much the sex, but his touch. Just being with Maxwell, brought her to physical and emotional ecstasy. She slowly opened her legs to him. She had to feel him inside of her. The walls of her vagina were throbbing with intense desire.

Maxwell had never in his life experienced such raw desire and acceptance. But tonight, within the confines of suite 2026, his lover taught him what true love felt like. Zolla's love validated that he had finally found love and peace, or had he? Maxwell skillfully positioned his throbbing tool, assuring limited pain as he prepared to enter his lover. Just then his body was brought to a complete halt. He could not move. Zolla sensed something was not right.

"Honey, what's wrong?"

"Zolla, sweetheart, I can't."

She blinked slowly, trying to digest his words. "What do you mean you can't? Is it me, Max? Have I done something wrong?"

Maxwell carefully repositioned the two of them, slowly bringing Zolla's body to rest on top of his. He wrapped his arms around her, while looking directly into her beautiful amber eyes. "Zolla, I can't share you. I just can't. Over the past few weeks I've done a tremendous amount of intense thinking."

"Intense thinking? I don't understand."

"Yes, thoughts about everything—you, me, Clayton, your childhood—and three issues continue to trouble me."

"What three issues?"

"Well; first is your childhood and how you were impacted. Second, your refusal to confront Clayton."

"My refusal to confront Clayton?" She raised her voice.

"Yes! Have you moved towards leaving Clayton?" All Zolla could do was give a sad look of disappointment. "See, I can't share you. I want to make love to my woman, my future wife, not Clayton's. I'm selfish. I will not share you. Finally, sweetheart, somewhere along our journey I developed compassion and empathy. You've been though a lot and I'm not trying to add to your pain. I don't want you to have any regrets and I'm not convinced that you won't."

Zolla felt her eyes welling up with tears. "Maxwell, baby, I love you."

"I know that. I don't doubt that at all. But sweetheart, I have to protect myself and dating you when you haven't given me any indication that you're going to leave Clayton, is no longer an option"

"Just give me time," Zolla pleaded. "Please give me time."

Out of frustration Maxwell elevated his voice. "Zolla, I can't, okay? I can't do it." He pushed away from her and began to get dressed.

Zolla was frantic. She could not believe what was unfolding before her eyes. She was overwhelmed with racing thoughts. She couldn't breath. She needed air. As she opened the doors to the terrace, the midnights crisp breeze gently swept across her damp face. She couldn't face him, so she stared across the way at the lights shining from the large white building.

"What does this mean? Where do we stand? Are you walking out of my life?" she whispered.

"Sweetheart, you never truly let me in," he said, matter-of-factly. "Look, I'm very direct. I've been very clear about my expectations. I will always love you, but, baby, be honest with yourself. You have decisions to make and they can't be made with me around. I have no choice but to go." He headed for the door. She returned to him and to the warmth provided by the fireplace.

"Maxwell, please. Please don't go. Please don't walk out on me." Zolla cried uncontrollably as she ran and hugged her true love. He took her into his arms and fought the urge to break down emotionally. He loved Zolla and wanted to spend the rest of his life with her but he refused to share her.

She stood before him in complete silence, stunned, with tears streaming from her eyes.

"You are a strong woman, Mrs. Ramsey, much stronger than you think. You'll be just fine. I love you and I always will." He looked at her beautiful face, wiped away her tears and kissed her passionately. Then he placed a single kiss on her forehead and departed.

Within the confines of suite 2026, Zolla's naked body collapsed onto the rug and she cried herself to sleep.

Chapter 14

"Grammy Knows Best"

As Maxwell drove home, he was consumed—consumed with haunting thoughts of his interaction with Zolla. Had he lost his mind? Was he insane or was he just a fuckin' idiot? How could he walk out on her? He had so many regrets. His guilt was unbearable. His thoughts were interrupted by the ringing of his cell phone.

"Garrison," he said in a no-nonsense tone.

"Bunny, is that you? It's your Grammy, baby."

"Yes, Grammy, it's me." He tried to soften his voice. He loved his maternal grandmother so much but he hated when she called him Bunny. Maxwell shook his head remembering how for years he had tried to persuade her against referring to him as Bunny. She even called him by his nickname at formal events. He had gotten the name because as a toddler he preferred to hop instead of walk and both grandparents thought the nickname to be very much fitting.

"Bunny, you sound different. Is everything all right?" There was complete silence. No he wasn't all right, but an in-depth discussion with his Grammy was not going to occur.

Maxwell's Grammy had reared him following his mother's, her darling daughter's untimely death. Maxwell's father had passed away several years earlier while on special assignment with the CIA. Grammy Henderson became his legal custodian while he was in his teens and she had made a vow to the Lord that he would be raised to follow in the footsteps of his father, grandfathers, and great grandfathers. They were very proud and honorable men. She had succeeded. Her bunny had done well for himself and they shared a very special bond. Bunny always referred to her as psychic because deep within her soul she could feel when Maxwell was in need of her candor and wisdom. Grammy never let him down.

"Look Bunny, I realize that you're this big shot lawyer and it's important for you to be tough and act like you don't have emotions. I'm here to tell you that you don't have to be that way with me. I'm your Grammy, and ever since your mother, my darling daughter passed, I've help raise you. I know you like the back of my hand. I also know that you have a heart of gold. Yeah, you're Mr. High and Mighty in that courtroom, but Bunny you have the most beautiful soul I have ever seen. Now, with that said, I want you, Maxwell Bartholomew Garrison...to tell me what exactly has you feeling so defeated."

Maxwell knew that when his Grammy said his entire name, she meant business, always had and always would. He wasn't about to break her perfect track record. In the past he had tried but never succeeded at his attempts to overthrow Grammy's determination to have her questions answered. On many occasions Maxwell even joked with colleagues of how his Grammy made Perry Mason and Colombo look like amateurs.

"Well, Grammy, I met this amazing woman."

"A woman? Lord, I should've known."

"No Grammy, this is different, very much so. From the moment I laid eyes on her, I felt something I had never felt before. I mean, she touched my soul."

"Do you love this woman?" Grammy peered at him through the receiver, he sensed her trying to read his expression.

"Yes."

"Well, Bunny, what's the problem?"

Maxwell paused, not certain if he should really share this information with his grandmother. "Well, uh, she's married."

Maxwell's Grammy was very strong; however, she was seldom surprised. The elevation of her tone gave way to her disapproval. "Married!"

"Yes, ma'am. At first it didn't matter to me that she was. I just had to have her. But, as my feelings grew more intense, I wanted her for myself. Sharing was not an option. I even gave her an ultimatum."

"How does she feel about you?"

"Well, I do believe she loves me, but she has a strong belief system against adultery. She even shared with me personal information about how her mother's infidelity destroyed her family. Her father walked away from his entire family. Grammy, allowing me to make love to her was completely out of the question. Imagine that. No woman has ever refused me. That is, not until Zolla. But tonight she was willing to abandon her values and give herself to me completely, and I refused her."

"I'm surprised. Bunny, you always have had a thing for beautiful women. I believe that's why you and that Lorissa divorced."

"Grammy, there you go again. I've already explained the horrible details. Lorissa and I were both unfaithful and unevenly yoked. We're both to blame for that disastrous marriage."

"Humph, I told you not to marry that uppity girl in the first place. Had her nose up in the air, acting all high and mighty. Boy, don't get Grammy started."

Maxwell had to laugh. "Grammy, can I finish?"

"Ok, baby. Grammy's listening."

"I've spent this entire month processing all the information Zolla told me pertaining to her life. I will not allow her to compromise her values at my expense and I will not change my stance either. I want her as mine, my woman, not Clayton's," he pouted.

Grammy was confused. "Who's Claytus?"

"Clayton, Grammy. He's her husband. Zolla is committed to sacrificing her happiness for a man who treats her as though her existence is irrelevant."

Maxwell could no longer contain his grief. He had to pull over and collect his thoughts.

"Bunny, are you crying? You are. Grammy never thought she would see the day, when a woman would walk into your life and touch your soul. No Lord, I never imagined that I, Nadine Henderson, would live to see this day. Listen Shugga, Grammy goin' share some very powerful words with you and I want you to listen closely. Shugga, God is in control of everything that is taking place in your life at this very moment, and if it's God's will that...Bunny what's that child's name?"

"Zolla. Zolla Ramsey," he beamed.

"If it's God's will that you and Zolla be together, then His will shall be done. Now, Grammy understands that right now it might be difficult for you to accept my words, but they're true. Grammy does know best. Zolla wasn't strong enough, so God gave you the courage to stand strong for the two of you. You had to walk away so she could grow and get her life in order."

"Grammy, this is torturous. Will this intense pain go away?"

"In time, all in time. Bunny, have faith and trust that God's will will be done. Pray and ask God to give you strength and He will. But most of all, never forget that God is in control of this situation, not you, not Zolla, but God, understand?"

"Yes ma'am."

"Ok, Shugga, listen, are you still coming to dinner next Sunday? Some of Grammy's hugs and home cooking will make you feel better. I'm thinking of making my Bunny's favorites— smothered chicken, rice, collard greens, candied yams, macaroni and cheese, potato salad, cornbread and peach tea."

Maxwell couldn't contain his excitement. He constantly bragged that his Grammy's cuisine was succulent; mouth-watering good.

"Chocolate bread pudding with rum sauce?"

"Of course, Bunny, of course."

"Grammy?"

"Yes, sweetie?"

"Thank you for your guidance, your strength and your love. You are my foundation. I hope you know how much I appreciate everything you've done for me."

"Now, you're making me cry. I better go. I love you and I'll see you Sunday. Bye, Bunny."

"Bye, Grammy."

As Maxwell pulled back into the flow of traffic, his cell phone rang. He was not surprised to see it was Zolla's number on the caller ID. The struggle to suppress his emotions was lost as he reflected on his Grammy's words of wisdom. *Zolla wasn't strong enough so God gave you the courage to stand strong for the two of you.* Maxwell turned off his cell and tossed it onto the passenger seat and drove home in complete silence. Nothing further needed to be stated. No more expectations.

Chapter 15

"A Misrepresentation of My True Self"

Today was not a good day, not at all. Zolla could not ascertain why she had come into the office. She was definitely not in the mood to see clients. Puffy red eyes revealed that she had spent the majority of the previous night crying. She had difficulty accepting the reality of all that had transpired between her and Maxwell. She had opened her soul to him, bearing all and stripping away remnants of shame, fear and guilt. In a moment of complete trust, she had laid her heart on the line. Had she lost him forever?

She had to pull herself together. It was noon and she was scheduled to meet with her client, Mrs. Harper, at two o'clock. While frantically searching in her upper right drawer for her Visine, she stumbled upon the letter she had crumpled, the letter she had received on the morning of February 7th, but could not stand to read in its entirety. This was the letter sent to her by her mother. Zolla slowly smoothed out the balled up letter while seating herself on the blue sofa. She hadn't shared any form of communication with her mother in seven months and she felt as though this letter was an attempt to bring healing to a relationship torn by the pain and shame of her mother's infidelity and deceit. She took several deep breaths as she cleared her thoughts and braced for her mother's words. In her heart she knew the time had come to face her mother's sordid past, not as a twelve-year-old child but as a woman. Yes, the time had come.

> *Dear Zolla,*
>
> *It's been far too long. I must admit my shame for allowing such distance, emotionally as well as physically, to occur between us. I carry the blame within my heart because this rift manifested during your childhood. You were only twelve*

years old. However, the pain left within my heart leaves me feeling as though what happened transpired within this very moment in time. Zolla, there is so much to share with you; many life lessons.

First, I need to apologize to you for what you saw when you and your father returned from Nanna's. I had no right to bring another man into your father's bed and for my daughter to be witness...

Zolla, from the bottom of my heart, I'm so sorry. I'm asking that you accept my apology. It's important to me that you understand that within my marriage there were multiple problems. To onlookers it appeared that William and I had a perfect marriage and that was far from the truth. I was a good actress. I learned how to normalize the dysfunction, and that's where I went wrong. Zolla, a woman or a man should never, under any circumstance, compromise their spirit. Your father did not love me in the manner I deserved to be loved. The only communication we shared was about finances or about you and

Zion. We seldom made love and during those rare occasions when we did, your father was only concerned with having his sexual appetite fed. You might be thinking, why did I not tell him what my needs were? Well, when I would approach William with my concerns, he would dismiss them as though they were irrelevant. As a result, my needs were silenced by me. I learned to mask my internal pain and my regrets. Until meeting Mitchell, I had been faithful to my marital vows. Zolla, you may find this difficult to understand, but, baby, my soul was thirsty. It needed to be energized. I wasn't searching for a replacement for your father when this wonderful man walked into my life. It's important to me that you know that I love Mitchell with all my heart. My love for him was real and it continues to be. It's also vital that my daughter remembers these words of wisdom from her mom:

1. Zolla, always be true to yourself. When all is said and done, integrity to one's self is priceless.

2. Never, and I mean never, under any circumstances, compromise your spirit. Never limit your emotional needs in order to enhance the emotional needs of others.

3. Never allow another to determine your worth. Your existence is priceless.

Within my marriage I became a mis-representation of my true self; allowing another to dictate my worth and significance as a wife, mother, damn it as a human being. I wanted you and Zion to posses the inner strength that eluded me. That's why I gave you names that began with the letter "Z." To me, the letter "Z" represents strength. All the angles are strong and precise. Each and every day I pray that you and your brother are happy.

I plan to see you and Zion during Christmas. Once again, I'm so very sorry for the pain I caused you. If I could change that day, I would. You, Zolla, are my first born, my baby girl, and a blessing to me. Be happy, be strong, be true to yourself and never be a misrepresentation of your true worth. Never compromise. Be the woman that I wasn't.

With all my love, your mother,
Narvella

Chapter 16

"No Regrets"

Maxwell had just wrapped up a meeting with his three partners. The entire staff was full of satisfaction as they celebrated their victorious triumph against one of Detroit's most powerful corporations. The class action was awarded $250,000,000. Although Maxwell was confident that an appeal would soon follow suit, it was a good day.

Sitting alone in his office, he felt more relaxed and his outlook on life was more positive. He contributed his heightened sense of awareness to the self-help books that

Zolla had forwarded to him following their initial encounter. She was feeling as though his attitude was in need of an adjustment.

It had been exactly two years since the horrific night—the night he closed the door, but not his heart, on Mrs. Ramsey. This tranquil moment was very much reflective of so many moments, countless days, endless hours when his thoughts were consumed with loving images of her. He often indulged in thoughts of what had become of her and Clayton. Had thoughts of him crossed her mind? Was he missed by her? Or had he become a vivid distortion of her past?

After their split, Maxwell sought sexual refuge in a manner that felt familiar. It was his attempt to self-medicate and heal his broken heart. But, he soon found himself comparing each of his lovers to Zolla, knowing full well that no one could measure up, and no one did. He was comfortable with his decision to abstain from actual relationships, courtships that went beyond sex. For the past six months Maxwell had simply consumed himself with work.

His thoughts were interrupted by a light knock on his office door. "Excuse me, Mr. Garrison."

"Yes, Lilly?"

Lillian Johnson was his very dedicated personal assistant. Each of the four partners shared combined staff consisting of a team of administrative assistants, paralegals, and legal aids.

However, each employed their own personal assistant.

"Mr. Garrison, you have a special delivery from Fed Ex."

"Thank you, Lilly."

"Mr. Garrison, once again, congratulations on your win."

"No, Lilly, this was a team collaboration. We all share in this victory." Lillian smiled as she departed from the office. "Have a nice weekend."

"Thank you," Lillian called.

As Maxwell's eyes slowly focused on the name listed on the upper left hand corner, his heart skipped a beat. He stood up and walked over to the window, still fingering the envelope in his hands. From his twenty-fifth floor view, Lake Michigan looked almost serene. He suddenly felt an emotion that had evaded him for years—fear. Without even thinking, he began to pace. He took deep breaths as he tried to regain his composure. Slowly, he walked back to his large oak desk, plopped down in the leather executive chair and carefully opened the envelope, which contained a letter. As he unfolded the paper he could smell faint likeness to her perfume.

He sighed. "Ok, Zolla, here I go."

Dear Maxwell,

I feel as though this letter is long overdue. Endless thoughts of you have crossed my mind within this past year. On countless occasions I've reached for the telephone or an ink pen to connect. However, something deep within my soul, each and every time, would intercept my desire. I do believe that my fear of being rejected by you again was the overwhelming guiding force.

Maxwell, has life been good to you? Are you happy? Please believe me when I say that your happiness is important to me. You are of importance to me. It is my hope that during these past two years thoughts of me have remained close to your heart. I've been well. My practice continues to thrive. Can you believe that I've had to refer new clients to colleagues? Yes, I've been blessed.

Just the other day I was sitting at the lake and

reflecting on how life can be filled with amazement. Amazing how you walked into my life and touched my heart and energized my soul. Who would have imagined that you, a man who I once loathed, were the one, the one that God had chosen as my soul mate. From the very moment my eyes settled on you in my office lobby, I just knew it. When I looked into your beautiful eyes, I saw it. And when you opened your mouth and your words reached out to me, I felt it.

However, what stood between you and I was time. Maxwell, our timing was off. Within my life there have been various complexities, first and foremost being unresolved issues stemming from my childhood. I carried the Scarlet Letter from my mother's tainted past. I want to thank you for demanding that I take a stand. I need to thank you for standing strong in your belief that we both deserved better. I want to say thank you for not accepting another man's wife into your bed. I want to honor you for being strong and walking away from love, so that I could grow. Even when my eyes were blind to what was *right, yours were open. And you had the courage to stand strong for the two of us.*

Maxwell, a very dear friend once told me that love is a state of grace. I recently went to my dictionary to seek out the meaning of grace. Grace is a sense of doing what is proper. I've come to learn that graceful intentions can leave one's heart in despair.

Yes, I have suffered. Maxwell, I miss you so very much. To preserve my sanity, I did what I had to do. I placed my pain in the hands of God. I prayed and I prayed. I prayed for God to take my pain away and in time it lessened. I prayed for God to give me insight, and in time my thoughts became less construed. I prayed for God to lessen my anger and increase my level of compassion so that I could forgive Clayton, you, my mother and, most of all, myself. I spent so much time on my knees in prayer, I developed bruised knees.

Never underestimate the power of God. Never underestimate his love and grace, and never forget how on one winter evening you walked into the life of a woman whose world was forever transformed by your presence. You gave me the courage to accept the reality that I deserved more, not financially but internally. My spirit was dehydrated. My soul was thirsty and only I could provide the nourishment. I had to take a stand. I had to be true to myself, so I walked away. Yes, Maxwell I walked away from the life that I shared with Clayton. I did it for myself and I did it for the daughters and sons I will have one day, if I'm blessed with children. And you know what? My heart is consumed with joy and I'm at peace. It doesn't matter what people think because when I look into the mirror, I like what I see. I see a woman who's at peace with herself.

Maxwell, thank you for your love, courage and friendship. I have no regrets. You are one of my many blessings. Be happy, stay close to God and love beyond measure. I Love You.

Zolla

Maxwell was speechless, full of emotion as he reflected on the truth: he had been missed by her. He sat in silence for what felt like hours, processing her words. He felt that his next course of action had been predetermined by a much higher power, as his right hand reached for his office phone.

"Yes, Mr. Garrison?" the receptionist asked cheerfully.

"Hey has Lilly departed?"

"Yes."

"Ok." As he placed the phone on the receiver, he knew that he could not trust this undertaking to just anyone. So he would phone his loyal assistant's voice mail with vital instructions. A slight smile played at the corners of his mouth as he again reached for his office phone with a renewed confidence.

"Lilly, first thing Monday morning, phone the florist and have seven dozen red roses delivered to Ms. Zolla Ramsey. Also, phone the Hyatt Hotel on Lake Shore and request the Presidential room, suite 2026."

A Reading Group Guide

A Misrepresentation of Myself

By Mary Gilder

About this Guide

The suggested questions should be utilized as a tool to help facilitate thought provoking group discussions.

Discussion Questions
(For my female and male readers)

1. Have you ever felt emotionally depleted?

2. After reading chapters one and two, can you on any level relate to Zolla's emotional crises?

3. Chapter five revealed all of the Ramsey's marital dysfunctions. After assessing Clayton's behavior, do you feel that he is a good husband? Do you feel that Zolla is being unreasonable?

4. What do you view as Clayton's strengths and what are his liabilities as a husband?

5. What is your opinion of Leena?

6. What is your opinion of Nia?

7. Both Leena and Nia love Zolla dearly and felt strong in their convictions as they pertained to Maxwell and Clayton. Which of the two friends gave Zolla the best advice and why?

8. What did you find appealing about Maxwell?

9. What about Maxwell's character did you find to appalling?

10. Was Maxwell wrong for insisting that Zolla walk away from her marriage?

11. Would you stay in a marriage for material gain if love, passion and respect for your mate was gone?

12. In the chapter titled "Suite 2026", were you shocked by Maxwell's decision? Did he make the right decision?

13. Were you moved by Zolla's mother's letter? What did you gain from it?

14. Did the ending shock you? How so?

15. Now that you have read the novel and had time to reflect on all dynamics, do you feel that Zolla should stay in her marriage? Before you address this question ask yourself, "Am I with my soul mate?"

16. The novel is titled A MISREPRESENTATION OF MYSELF. What do you believe the title is conveying to the reader?

17. Identify the wisdom you gained from the reading of this novel?

18. Leena in Chapter eight told Zolla that if she could not look in life's mirror and be true to herself, then she was living a lie. How will you ensure from this point forward you honor your spirit?

19. Finally, the most thought provoking question, have you ever encountered a "FUCK KA MAN" or a "FUCK KA WOMAN"?

Be good to yourself,
And love abundantly,
Mary E. Gilder

Word of Hello

I would like to extend a word of hello to my readers as I share with you the joy consumed within my heart as I reflect on this amazing journey. For as far back as I can recall, I've shared numerous passions however, what I am most passionate about is my love of the written word and giving life to my creative thoughts.

You have just read the benefactor of my amazing literary journey. It is my hope that this fascinating read encourages you to focus on what is most important in the end by asking how the following manifest within your heart: Love, Greed, Faith, Compassion, Selfishness, Joy, Fear, Hope and did I mention LOVE…

When all is said and done did my readers learn the life lessons they were sent here to learn.

I do believe that you are all in for a wondrous literary experience as you follow the complexities of my many unforgettable characters. I so look forward to this amazing literary journey with you.

Don't short change you heart,

Mary E. Gilder

About the Author

Mary E. Gilder was born and reared in the beautiful city of San Diego, California. A proud graduate of Samuel Morse High School, she went on to earn a Bachelor of Science and a Masters Degree in Clinical Social Work from San Diego State University. As well as, recognition form the National Association of Women, for her scholarly achievements.

Along with being an Author, Mary is also a Licensed Clinical Therapist, Consultant, Human Rights Activist and Speaker. Mary's greatest passion is focused on creating literary work that will provoke reflective thought and creative energy by challenging our core beliefs. Her hope is that from this process, her readers will be encouraged to live a life that will produce no regrets.

Mary resides in lovely Northern, California with her family and has just completed her second novel.

Visit her website at www.maryegilder.com.

Also, visit her love discussion site at L-is4Love.com.